Linda Alexander
5 0 - 36TH St.

Union City

New Jersey

THE BOBBSEY TWINS

THE BOBBSEY TWINS BOOKS

By Laura Lee Hope

"Oh!" screamed Freddie, "Snoop has gone up with the kite!"

The Bobbsey Twins

The Bobbsey Twins

By

LAURA LEE HOPE

GROSSET & DUNLAP
Publishers   New York

The Bobbsey Twins

PREFACE TO THE NEW EDITION

YOU CHILDREN MAY NOT AGREE, but it seems to me that the biggest difference between children like Freddie and Flossie, and Nan and Bert, and older folk is in their attitude toward the passing of time. It seems to move painfully slowly for you children, but oh, how the years fly past for your fathers and mothers and grandfathers and grandmothers!

I was reminded by my publishers some time ago that it is well over forty years since the first Bobbsey story was written and published. But what brought that fact forcibly to my mind was something that happened a few days ago. I was reading aloud to a little girl who lives next door and who often comes in to visit me and to sample my ginger cookies, just as her grandmother used to come over when I was writing the early Bobbsey books and ask me to read the chapters as they were finished.

We were reading the last chapter of THE

BOBBSEY TWINS—"Merry Days Indoors and Out," as it used to be called. The twins were giving a party and one of Bert's friends was showing magic lantern slides to the enraptured guests.

"What's a magic lantern, Miss Hope?" asked my little neighbor. She never had heard of such a device which we used to think was so marvelous a half-century ago. And why should she? After all, this is the age of television. Magic lanterns belong to the dark ages when people got about by horse and carriage or horse and cutter and there were no such wonders as electric refrigerators or vacuum cleaners. Can you believe it?

I began to see what my publishers had been hinting at—that there is a great deal in the original edition of the book you are about to read that you never saw or perhaps even heard about. So in the new edition I have made a few changes— not in Freddie or Flossie or Nan or Bert, but in some of their surroundings. Before I made them I took up each change with my young neighbor. She gave her approval to each one of them, and I sincerely hope that all of you will feel the same way about it.

LAURA LEE HOPE

CONTENTS

THE BOBBSEY TWINS

CHAPTER I

THE BOBBSEY TWINS AT HOME

IT WAS Saturday morning and the Bobbsey twins were very busy. They were all seated around the dining-room table, making houses and furnishing them. The houses were made out of cardboard shoe boxes, and had square holes cut in them for doors, and other smaller holes for windows.

Inside the little houses were cardboard chairs and tables, and bits of dress material for carpets and rugs. Pieces of tissue paper were pasted on the windows for curtains.

Three of the houses were long and low, but Bert had placed his box on one end and divided it into five stories, and Flossie said she thought it looked exactly like a "department" house.

"You mean *apartment* house," said Nan, smiling at her little sister.

There were four of the twins. Now that sounds

funny, doesn't it? But, you see, there were two sets. Bert and Nan were twelve years old, and Freddie and Flossie were almost six.

Nan was a tall and slender girl, with a dark complexion and red cheeks. Her eyes were a deep brown and so were the curls that clustered around her head.

Bert was indeed a twin, not only because he was the same age as Nan, but because he looked so very much like her. To be sure, he looked like a boy, while she looked like a girl, but he had the same dark complexion, the same brown eyes and hair, and his voice was very much the same, only stronger.

Freddie and Flossie were just the opposite of their older brother and sister. Each was short and chubby, with a fair, round face, light-blue eyes and fluffy golden hair.

Sometimes Daddy Bobbsey called Flossie his little Fat Fairy, which always made her laugh. But Freddie didn't want to be called a fairy, so his daddy called him the Fat Fireman, which pleased him very much, and made him rush around the house shouting:

"Fire! Fire! Here comes the hook and ladder! Get out of the way, everybody!" in a manner that seemed very lifelike. During the past year Freddie had seen two fires, and the exciting work of the firemen had thrilled him.

The Bobbsey family lived in the town of Lakeport, situated at the head of Lake Metoka, a clear and beautiful sheet of water upon which the twins loved to go boating. Mr. Richard Bobbsey was a lumber merchant, with a large yard and dock on the lake shore, and a saw and planing mill close by.

Their house was a quarter of a mile away, on a quiet, pretty street and had a small but nice garden around it. In the rear was a garage, on the second floor of which the children loved to play.

"I'm going to cut out a fancy tablecloth for my dining-room table," said Nan. "It's going to be the finest tablecloth that ever was."

"Nice as Aunt Emily's?" questioned Bert. "She's got a—a beauty, all embroidered with roses."

"This is going to be white, like the window curtains," replied Nan.

While Freddie and Flossie watched her with deep interest, she took a small square of tissue paper and folded it up several times. Then she cut curious-looking holes in the folded piece with a pair of sharp scissors. When the paper

was unfolded once more a lovely pattern appeared.

"Oh, how bee-yootiful!" cried Flossie. "Make
me one, Nan!"

"And me, too," put in Freddie. "I want a real
red one," and he brought forth a bit of red pin-
wheel paper he had been saving.

"Oh, Freddie, let me have the red paper for
my stairs," cried Bert.

"No, I want a tablecloth, like Nan. You take
the white paper."

"Whoever saw white paper on a stairs—I
mean white carpet," said Flossie.

"I'll give you a marble for the paper, Freddie," Bert coaxed.

But Freddie shook his head. "Want a tablecloth, nice as Aunt Em'ly," he answered. "Going
to set a flower on the table too!" he added, and
ran out of the room.

When he came back he had a flowerpot in his
hand half the size of his house, with a big red
feather from an old Indian costume stuck in the
dirt for a flower.

"Oh, look! How funny," cried Nan, and burst
out laughing. "Oh, Freddie, how will we ever
set that big flowerpot on such a little cardboard
table?"

"I can set it there!" declared the little fellow.

Before Nan could stop him the flowerpot went up and the cardboard table came down and was mashed flat.

"Hey! Freddie's breaking up housekeeping!" cried Bert.

"Oh, Freddie, do take the flowerpot away!" begged Flossie. "It's too big to go into the house anyway."

Freddie looked perplexed for a moment. Then he said: "I'm going to play garden around the house. This is a—a lilac tree!" And he set the flowerpot down close to Bert's elbow.

Bert was very busy trying to put a cardboard chimney on his house and did not notice the pot. A moment later Bert's elbow hit the flowerpot and down it went on the floor, breaking into several pieces and scattering the dirt over the rug.

"Oh, Bert! what have you done?" cried Nan. "Get the broom and the dustpan before Dinah comes."

"It was Freddie's fault."

"Oh, my lilac tree is all gone!" cried the little boy. "And my fireplug too," he added, referring to the flowerpot, which he had used the day before when playing fireman.

At that moment, Dinah, the cook, came in from the kitchen.

"Well, I declare to gracious!" she exclaimed.

"If you children ain't gone an' mussed up the floor again!"

"Bert broke my hydrant!" said Freddie, and he began to cry.

"Oh, never mind, Freddie, there are plenty of other pots in the cellar," declared Nan. "It was an accident, Dinah," she added.

"Everything that happens in this house is an accident," grumbled Dinah, as she went off to get the dustpan and broom.

As soon as the dirt and the broken flowerpot had been cleared away, Nan cut out the red table-cloth for Freddie, which made him forget the loss of the "lilac tree" and the "hydrant."

"Let us make a row of houses," suggested Flossie. "Bert's big house can be at the head of the street."

This suggestion was carried out. Fortunately, more cardboard boxes were to be had, and from these the children made shade trees and some benches. Bert even cut out what he said was a moving van and placed it before one of the houses. In the van was a tiny cardboard piano. When the work was complete they called Dinah in to admire it, which she did standing near the doorway with her fat hands resting on her broad hips.

"Well, I declare, it certainly does look real,"

said the cook. "It's a wonder to me how you children can make such things."

"We learned it in Miss Greene's kindergarten class when we were as little as Freddie and Flossie," replied Nan.

"Yes, in the kindergarten," put in Flossie.

"But we don't make fire engines there," complained Freddie.

At this Dinah began to laugh, shaking from head to foot.

"Fire engines, Freddie? Reckon you're goin' to be a fireman when you're a man, hey?"

"Yes, I'm going to be a real fireman," was the ready answer.

"An' what are you goin' to be, Master Bert?"

"Oh, I'm going to be a flyer," said Bert.

"I want to be a flyer, too," put in Freddie. "A flyer and a fireman."

"Oh dear, I wouldn't want to be a pilot and go up in the sky so high," said Nan.

"Well, then you can get married," suggested Freddie. "Or you can get to be a sten'grapher or something like that."

"You mean stenographers, Freddie. I'm going to be a stenographer when I get big."

"I don't want to be any stenogerer," put in Flossie. "I'm going to keep a candy store, and have all the candy I want, and ice cream—"

"Me too!" burst in Freddie. "I'm going to have a candy store, an' be a fireman, an' a flyer, all together!"

"Dear! dear!" Dinah laughed. "Just listen to him! It's wonderful what you're goin' to do when you're big."

At that moment the front doorbell rang, and all rushed to the hallway to greet their mother, who had been downtown on a shopping tour.

CHAPTER II

A BAD FRIGHT

"OH, MOTHER, what did you bring?" cried the twins, as they gathered around Mrs. Bobbsey in the hallway. She had several small packages in her hands, and one looked very much like a box of candy.

Mrs. Bobbsey kissed them all before speaking. "Have you been good while I was gone?" she asked.

"I guess we tried to be good," answered Bert doubtfully.

"Freddie's hydrant got broke, that's all," said Flossie. "Dinah swept up the dirt."

Before anything more could be told all were in the dining room and Mrs. Bobbsey was called upon to admire the row of houses. Then the box of candy was opened and each twin received a piece.

"Now you had better go out and play," said their mother. "Dinah wants to set the table for dinner. But be sure and put on your heavy coats. It is very cold and feels like snow."

"Oh, if only it would snow!" said Bert. He was anxious to try a sled he had received the Christmas before.

Being Saturday, there was no school, so all the boys and girls of the neighborhood were out playing. Some of the girls were skipping rope, and Nan joined them, while Bert went off to join a crowd of boys playing football.

There were only fifteen boys to make up two teams, so the boys had to divide into two sides of seven players each. This left one boy over.

"What am I going to do?" asked the boy left over, who was named Jack Barton. "I want to play, too."

"You can be the cheerleader," suggested one small boy who wore a leather helmet much too big for him.

"I don't want to be that."

"I'll tell you what you can do," suggested Bert. "You can be the referee."

"I've got to have a whistle for that."

"I'll lend you my whistle," said the boy who had been chosen to be the captain of one of the sides. He brought from his pocket a bright, silver whistle.

"All right, I'll be the referee," said Jack.

"And you have got to mind what I say or I'll put you out of the game," he went on sternly.

The game was soon in full swing. Of course, the boys played in their own fashion and not strictly according to rules, and the referee had to warn them any number of times.

By the time the game was half over the score stood 18 to 30 and Bert was on the losing side.

"We've got to brace up," said the captain of Bert's side. "Everybody do his best."

"That's what I've been doing right along," said one boy.

"Well, try and do better."

"We're too slow in passing the ball," said Bert. "Everybody get a move on."

The game went on and slowly but surely Bert's side began to gain until the score stood at 30 to 36.

"We've only got six minutes more to play," said a boy on Bert's side. "Let's smash into 'em!"

The game went on until they had only two minutes more to play.

"A tie! A tie!" was the sudden cry. And it was true—the score was now a tie, 36 to 36.

The football went into play again. Bert caught it and away he ran down the field. Several boys tried to catch him, but he dodged them all and carried it over the goal line.

"Touchdown!" cried Bert's teammates.

A moment later the game came to an end with Bert's team the winners.

In the meantime Freddie and Flossie had gone down near the Bobbsey garage.

"Let's play horse," suggested Freddie to Flossie. They had reins of red leather, with bells, and Freddie was the horse while his twin sister was the driver.

"I'm a naughty horse. I'll run away if you don't watch me," cautioned Freddie, and began to prance around wildly, against the grape arbor and then up against the side fence.

"Whoa! Whoa!" screamed Flossie, jerking on the reins. "Whoa, you naughty horse! If I had a whip, I'd beat you!"

"If you did that, I'd kick," answered Freddie, and he began to kick up his heels in the air. He finally settled down, though, and ran around just as nicely as any horse could. Then he snorted and ran up to a pail of water standing near the garage, and Flossie pretended to give him a drink and some hay, and unharnessed him just as if he were a real horse.

Nan, playing with her friends, was counting while another girl named Grace Lavine jumped rope. Grace was a great jumper and already had passed forty when her mother called to her from the window.

"Grace, don't jump so much. You'll get over-tired."

"Oh, no, I won't," returned Grace. She was a headstrong girl and always wanted to have her own way.

"But jumping gave you a headache only last week," continued Mrs. Lavine. "Now, don't do too much of it," and then she closed the window and went back to her interrupted work.

"Oh dear, Mother made me trip," sighed Grace. "I don't think that was fair."

"But your mother doesn't want you to jump any more," said another friend, Nellie Parks.

"Oh, she didn't say that. She said not to jump too much."

It was now Nan's turn to jump and she went up to twenty-seven and then tripped. Nellie followed and reached thirty-five. Then came another girl who jumped to fifty-six.

"I'm going to a hundred this time," said Grace, as she skipped into place.

"Oh, Grace, you'd better not!" cried Nan.

"You're afraid I'll beat you," declared Grace.

"No, I'm not. But your mother said—"

"I don't care what she said. She didn't forbid

my jumping," cut in the obstinate girl. "Are you going to turn the rope or not?"

"Yes, I'll turn," replied Nan, and at once the jumping started. Soon Grace had reached forty. Then came fifty, and then sixty.

"I do believe she will reach a hundred after all," declared Nellie Parks, a little enviously.

"I will, if you turn steadily," answered Grace, in a panting voice. Her face was strangely pale.

"Oh, Grace, hadn't you better stop?" asked Nan. She was a little frightened, but, nevertheless, kept on turning the rope.

"No!" puffed Grace. "Go—go on!"

She had now reached eighty-five. Nellie Parks was counting:

"Eighty-six, eighty-seven, eighty-eight, eighty-nine, ninety!" She went on, "Ninety-one, ninety-two—"

"No—not so—so fast!" panted Grace. "I—I—oh!"

And then, just as Nellie was counting "ninety-seven," Grace sank down in a heap, her eyes closed and her face as white as a sheet.

For a moment the other girls looked on in blank wonder, not knowing what to do.

"Oh, girls, she has fainted!" Nan cried.

"Perhaps she is dead!" burst out Nellie. "And if she is, we killed her, for we turned the rope!"

"Oh, Nellie, please don't say that!" said Nan. She could scarcely speak the words.

"Shall I go and tell Mrs. Lavine?" asked another girl who stood near.

"No—yes," answered Nan. She was so bewildered she scarcely knew what to say. "Oh, isn't it awful!"

They gathered close around the fallen girl, but nobody dared to touch her. While they were there, and one girl had gone to tell Mrs. Lavine, a tall man came up. It was Mr. Bobbsey, coming home from the lumber yard for lunch.

"What is the trouble?" he asked, and then saw Grace. "What happened to Grace?"

"She was—was jumping rope, and couldn't jump any more," sobbed Nan. "Oh, Daddy, she —isn't d-dead, is she?"

Mr. Bobbsey was startled and with good reason, for he had heard of more than one little girl being overcome from too much jumping. He took the limp little girl in his arms and hurried to the Lavine house with her.

"Run and get Dr. Briskett," Mr. Bobbsey shouted back to Nan.

Dr. Briskett lived but a short block away, and Nan ran as fast as her legs could carry her. The doctor had just come in from making his morning calls and still had his hat and overcoat on.

"Oh, Dr. Briskett, do come at once!" she sobbed. "Something terrible has happened to Grace Lavine, and we did it, turning the rope for her!"

"Where is she?" the doctor asked, dumfounded.

"Daddy just carried her into her house."

Without waiting to hear more, Dr. Briskett headed for the Lavine house, around which quite a crowd had now collected. In the crowd was Bert.

"Is Grace really dying?" he asked.

"I—I—hope not," answered Nan. "Oh, Bert, it's dreadful! I was turning the rope and she had reached ninety-seven, when all at once she sank down, and—" Nan's voice trembled and she could not go on.

"You girls are crazy to jump rope so much," said a big boy named Danny Rugg. Danny was something of a bully and very few of the girls liked him.

"It's no worse than playing football," Nellie Parks snapped.

"Yes, it is, much worse," retorted Danny. "Rope jumping brings on heart disease. I heard my father say so."

"I hope Grace didn't get heart disease," sobbed Nan.

"You turned the rope," went on Danny maliciously. "If she dies, they'll put you in prison, Nan Bobbsey."

"They will not!" cried Bert, coming to his sister's rescue. "I won't let them. Nan didn't mean to hurt Grace."

"You can't stop 'em, Bert Bobbsey."

"Can't I?"

"No, you can't."

"I'll see if I can't," answered Bert, and he gave Danny such a look that the latter edged away, thinking Bert might punch him.

Dr. Briskett had gone into the house and the crowd hung around impatiently, waiting for news. The excitement increased, and Mrs. Bobbsey arrived, followed by Freddie and Flossie, who had just finished playing horse.

"Nan, Nan! Whatever happened?" cried Mrs. Bobbsey.

"Oh, Mother!" sobbed Nan, and burst into tears in her mother's arms.

Just then Mr. Bobbsey came from Grace Lavine's house. Seeing his wife comforting their daughter, he hurried up to them.

"Grace will be all right," he announced. "She had a fainting spell, that is all. But I think after this she had better leave rope skipping alone."

CHAPTER III

THE FIRST SNOWSTORM

NAN felt greatly relieved to learn that Grace was going to be all right.

"Oh, Mother, I am so glad!" she said, over and over again.

"I am glad, too," answered Mrs. Bobbsey. "Grace's mother has told her several times not to jump so much."

"Yes, I heard her." Nan's eyes dropped. "I shouldn't have turned the rope for her."

In the end Nan told her mother the whole story, to which Mrs. Bobbsey listened very gravely.

"It was certainly wrong, Nan," she said. "After this I hope my little girl will try to use better judgment."

"I will try," promised Nan.

It was long after the dinner hour before the excitement died away. Then it was learned that Grace was resting quietly and that the doctor

18

had ordered that she be kept quiet for several days. She was very much frightened and had told her parents that she would never disobey them again.

The time was the fall of the year, and that Saturday evening there was a feeling in the air that promised snow.

"Oh, if only it would snow!" exclaimed Bert, several times. "I like winter best of all."

"I don't," answered Nan. "Think of the nice flowers we have in the summer."

"You can't have much fun with flowers, Nan."

"Yes, you can. And think of the birds—"

"I like the summer," piped up Freddie, " 'cause then we go to the country where the cows and chickens are!"

"Yes, and gather the eggs," put in Flossie. She had gathered eggs many times during the past summer, while on a visit to their Uncle Daniel Bobbsey's farm at Meadow Brook. All the Bobbsey children thought Meadow Brook the finest country place in all the world.

Bert's wish for snow was soon gratified. Sunday morning found it snowing steadily, the soft flakes coming down silently and covering the ground to the depth of several inches.

"Winter has come at last!" cried the boy. "Hurrah!"

"The snow is not quite deep enough for sledding yet," returned his father.

Despite the storm, all four children and Mrs. Bobbsey went to Sunday school in the morning. Mr. Bobbsey said he would meet them at church later on.

To the children, traveling back and forth through the snow was great sport. Bert, in spite of his best gloves, made several large snowballs and threw them at the other boys. The other boys threw some back in return and Bert's hat was knocked off.

It might have become open warfare had not Mrs. Bobbsey intervened.

All through that night the snow continued to come down, and on Monday morning it was more than a foot deep. The air was crisp and cold, and all of the children felt in the best of spirits.

"Nan and Bert can go to school," said Mrs. Bobbsey. "But I think Freddie and Flossie had better stay home. Walking through this snow would be too hard on them."

"I want to go out in the snow!" cried Freddie. "I don't want to stay indoors all day."

"You shall go out later on, in the back yard," promised his mother.

"They can watch Sam shovel off the snow," put in Mr. Bobbsey.

Sam, who was Dinah's husband, was the Bobbseys' handyman.

"Yes, let us watch him!" cried Flossie.

Soon she and Freddie were at the window, watching the colored man as he banked up the snow on either side of the garden walk and the sidewalk. Once Sam made a motion as if to throw a shovelful of snow at the window, and this made the little twins dodge back in alarm and then laugh heartily.

"I know what let's do!" cried Flossie presently.

"What?" demanded Freddie.

"Let us get some really truly clean snow and make ice cream."

"Let's!" burst out her twin. "Let us make a— a ton of it and then we can pretend that I have an ice-cream store and you can come and buy from me."

"Will you make choc'late ice cream?" asked Flossie. Chocolate ice cream was her favorite.

"Sure—I'll make vanilla, an' choc'late, an' strawberry, an' ev'rything," declared Freddie.

Dinah gave the children several small tin cups and a bowl. She also let them have a little sugar and some chocolate syrup. Then, from Sam, they got the clean snow, taken from a spotless white drift he had not touched with his shovel.

"Now, you let me help make ice cream," insisted Flossie.

"But you got to buy it," objected Freddie.

"Well, I'm going to be a—a clerk first and help make it," said the little girl.

So the little twins set to work in a corner of the kitchen to make their ice cream. Dinah watched them.

"Don't you mess up my floor," she cautioned. "An' don't eat that stuff—unless you want a stomach-ache," she added.

"Oh, can't we eat a little?" pleaded Flossie.

"Just a taste, child—just a taste."

Soon the so-called ice cream was finished— plain white, which the twins called vanilla, one with a few drops of strawberry juice, and one with the chocolate syrup.

Then Freddie pretended to sell it at fifty cents a quart—and Flossie bought all three kinds, paying two buttons each time. It was lots of fun. But both children were careful to mind Dinah and ate only a little bit, for neither of them wanted to get sick.

The school was only a few blocks away from the Bobbsey home, but Nan and Bert had all they could do to reach it, for the wind had made the snow drift, so that in some spots it was very deep.

"Better look out or we'll get in over our heads," cried Bert.

"Oh, Bert," answered his twin sister. "How would we ever get out?"

"Yell for help and have the street-cleaning men dig us out," he said merrily. "Nan, I just love the snow. It makes me feel like singing and whistling." And he broke into a merry whistle.

"I love it because it looks so white and clean, Bert."

They were speedily joined by a number of other boys and girls, all bound for school. Some of the girls were having fun washing each other's faces with the snow, and it was not long before Nan had her face washed too. The cold snow on her cheek and ear did not feel very nice, but it was a lot of fun and, laughing and shouting, Nan proceeded to wash another girl's face in turn.

The boys were already snowballing each other, some on one side of the street and some on the other. The snowballs were flying in all directions and Bert was hit on the back and on the shoulder.

"I'll pay you back!" he cried to Charley Mason, who had hit him in the back, and he let fly a snowball which landed directly on Charley's neck. Some of the snow went down Charley's back and made him shiver from the cold.

"I wouldn't stand for that, Charley," said Danny Rugg, who was close at hand. "I'd let him have it right in the face, if I were you."

"You let him have it," grumbled Charley. "You can throw awfully straight."

Danny prided himself on his throwing, which, however, was not much better than the throwing of the other boys. He quickly made two hard snowballs. With one of these in each hand he ran out into the street and waited until Bert's hands were empty. Then he came up still closer and threw one of the snowballs with all his might. Bert ducked, but the snowball struck him in the back of the head and sent him staggering.

"Hi, how do you like that?" roared Danny in high glee. "Have another?"

As Bert stood up and looked around, Danny let fly again, this time hitting Bert directly in the ear. The snowball was so hard it made Bert cry out in pain.

"Shame on you, Danny Rugg, to hit Bert so hard as that!" cried Nan, who was watching.

"Oh, you keep still, Nan Bobbsey!" retorted Danny. "This is our game, not yours."

"But you shouldn't have come so close before you threw the snowball."

"I know what I'm doing," growled the big boy, but he ran off when he saw Bert's angry face.

The whack on Bert's ear made it ache, and he did not feel nearly so full of fun when he entered the schoolyard. Several of his friends came up to him in sympathy.

"Does it hurt you very much, Bert?" asked one.

"Not much now," said Bert. "But it wasn't fair of Danny to come so close, or to make the snowballs so hard."

"Let's duck Danny in the snow," suggested one of the boys.

Everybody thought this a good plan, but nobody wanted to start it, for, as I have said before, Danny was a good deal of a bully, and could get very rough at times.

While the boys were talking the matter over, the school bell rang and all had to go to their classrooms. In a little while Bert's ear stopped aching, but he did not forget how Danny Rugg had treated him.

"I'll pay him back when we go home to lunch," Bert told himself, and laid his plans accordingly.

As soon as Bert got out of school he hurried

into a corner of the yard and made three good, hard snowballs. These he concealed under his jacket and then waited for Danny to appear.

The big boy must have known that Bert would try to square matters with him. As soon as he came out he ran in the direction of one of the main streets of Lakeport, just the opposite direction to that which he usually took.

"You're not getting away from me!" cried Bert, and ran after him. He let one snowball fly and it landed on Danny's back. Then he threw another and knocked off the bully's cap.

"Hey! Stop that!" roared Danny, and stooped to pick up the cap. Whiz! came the third snowball and hit Danny on the cheek. He let out a cry of pain.

"I'll fix you for that, Bert Bobbsey!" he yelled, stooping down in the street. "How do you like that?"

He had picked up a large chunk of ice lying in the gutter, and now he threw it at Bert's head with all his might. Bert dodged, and the ice went sailing past him and hit the display window of a small shoe store. The big pane of glass was shattered into a hundred pieces!

CHAPTER IV

THE BROKEN WINDOW

NEITHER Danny nor Bert had expected such an ending to their snowball fight and for the moment neither knew what to do. Then, as the owner of the shoe store came running out, both set off on a run.

"Stop! stop!" roared the shoe store proprietor, coming after them. "Stop, I say!"

But the more he shouted the harder they ran. Both soon reached the corner, and while Danny went up the side street, Bert went down, so the boys soon became widely separated.

Reaching the corner, the owner of the store did not know which boy to go after, but made up his mind to follow Bert, who could not run as fast as Danny. So after Bert he came, with such long strides that he was soon close to the boy.

Bert was terrified, for he was afraid that if he

were caught he might be arrested. Seeing an alleyway leading to the right, he ducked into it. At the rear was a fence, and with all speed he climbed up and let himself down on the other side. Then he dodged swiftly around a corner, through another alleyway, and into the street leading home.

The shoe dealer might have followed, but he suddenly remembered that he had left the store unprotected and that somebody might come in and run off with his stock and his money. So he returned to his shop in a hurry; and the chase came to an end.

When Bert got home he was all out of breath, and his legs trembled so that he could scarcely stand. Nan had just arrived and the family were preparing to sit down to lunch.

"Why, Bert, why do you run so hard?" protested his mother. "We are glad you tried to be in time for lunch, but next time please allow yourself more time."

"Oh, I—I'm all right," Bert panted. He started to drop into his seat, but Mrs. Bobbsey made him go upstairs and wash his hands and comb his hair.

Poor Bert was in a fever of anxiety all through the meal. Every instant he expected to hear the front doorbell ring, and find a policeman there to take him to the police station. He could scarcely eat a mouthful.

"What's the matter, Bert? Do you feel sick?" asked his father.

"No, I'm not sick," he answered.

"You play altogether too hard. Take it easy. The snow will last a long time," went on Mr. Bobbsey.

After lunch Bert dreaded to go back to school. But he could think of no excuse for staying in the house and at last set off in company with Nan. He looked around for Danny, but the big boy did not show himself.

"What's the matter with you, Bert?" questioned his twin sister, as they trudged along.

"Nothing is the matter, Nan."

"But there is. You act so strange."

"I—I don't feel very well."

"Then you did run too hard, after all."

"It wasn't that, Nan." Bert looked around him. "Do you see anything of Danny Rugg?"

"No." Nan stopped short. "Bert Bobbsey, did you have a fight with him?"

"No—that is, not a real fight. I chased him with some snowballs and he threw a big chunk of ice at me."

"Did he hit you?"

"No, he—he—oh, Nan, perhaps I had better

tell you. But you must promise not to tell anybody else."

"Tell me what?"

"Will you promise not to tell?"

"Yes," said Nan promptly, for she and her twin brother always trusted each other.

"When Danny threw the ice at me it flew past and broke Mr. Ringley's window."

"What, the shoe window?"

"Yes. Mr. Ringley came running out after us. I ran one way and Danny ran another, and Mr. Ringley followed me. I ran into the alleyway past Jackson's place, and got over the fence, and he didn't come any farther."

"Does Mr. Ringley think you broke the window?"

"I guess he must, because he followed me and not Danny."

"But you had nothing to do with it. Oh, Bert, what made you run away at all? Why didn't you stop and tell the truth?"

"I—I got scared, that's why. I was afraid he'd call a policeman."

"Danny ought to own up that he did it."

"He won't do it. He'll blame it on me if he can—because I chased him in the first place."

"Did Mr. Ringley know who you are?"

"I don't know. Now, Nan, remember, you promised not to tell."

"All right, Bert, I won't say a word. But—but—what do you think Mr. Ringley will do?"

"I don't know."

When they reached the school, Danny Rugg was nowhere to be seen. The boys continued to have fun snowballing, but Bert had no heart for play and went to his classroom immediately. But he could not put his mind on his lessons and gave the wrong answer both in geography and arithmetic.

"Bert, you are not paying attention," said the teacher severely. "You just said the capital of Pennsylvania was Albany. You must know better than that."

"Harrisburg," corrected Bert.

"After this, pay more attention."

Danny Rugg did not come back to school, nor did he show himself until an hour after school was out. Bert had gone home and brought out his sled, and he and Nan were giving Freddie and Flossie a ride around the block when Danny hailed Bert.

"Come here, I want to talk to you," he called, from across the street.

"What do you want?" asked Bert cautiously.

"I've got something to tell you. It won't take but a minute."

Bert hesitated, and then leaving Nan to go on alone with the sled, he crossed to where Danny was standing, partly sheltered by a tree.

"You can't blame that broken window on me, Danny Rugg," Bert began hotly.

"Not so loud!" whispered Danny in alarm. "I'm not going to blame it on you, Bert. I only want you to promise to keep quiet about it."

"Why should I? It was your fault."

"Was it? I don't think so. You began the fight. Besides, if you dare say a word, I'll—I'll give you a thrashing!" blustered Danny.

He clenched his fists as he spoke and looked so fierce that Bert retreated a step.

"I haven't said anything, Danny."

"Then you had better not. Old Ringley doesn't know who broke his window. So you keep quiet. Do you hear?"

"Are you sure he doesn't know?"

"Yes, because he has been asking everybody about it."

There was a pause and the two boys looked at each other.

"You ought to pay for the window," said Bert.

"Huh! I'm not going to do it. You can pay for it if you want to. But don't you dare say anything about me! If you do, you'll catch it, and don't you forget it!" And then Danny walked off.

"What did he have to say?" questioned Nan, when Bert came back to her.

"He wants me to keep still. He says Mr. Ringley doesn't know who did it."

"Did you promise to keep still, Bert?"

"No, but if I say anything Danny says he'll fight me."

A crowd of boys and girls now came up and the talk was changed. All were having a merry time in the snow, and for the time being Bert forgot his troubles. He and Nan gave Freddie and Flossie a fast ride which pleased the younger twins very much.

"I wish you were really and truly horses," said Flossie. "You go so bee-yootiful!"

"And if I had a whip I could make you go faster," put in Freddie.

"Why, Freddie Bobbsey!" exclaimed Nan. "Would you hit the horse that gave you such a nice ride?"

"Let me give you a ride," answered the little fellow, to change the subject.

He insisted upon it, and soon Nan was on the sled behind Flossie, and Bert and Freddie were hauling them along over the level snow where pulling was easy. This was great sport for Freddie, and he puffed and snorted like a real horse, and kicked up his heels, very much to Flossie's delight.

"Giddap!" shrieked the little girl. "Giddap!" and moved back and forth on the sled, to make it go faster. Away went Freddie and Bert, as fast as the legs of the smaller twin could travel.

"Oh, this is fun!" cried Nan in delight.

"Go faster!" shrieked Flossie.

"I—now—I can't!" panted poor Freddie. "It's so—so slippery."

He had scarcely spoken when both feet went out from under him. Luckily Bert quickly pulled the sled to one side, or the little fellow would have been struck and possibly hurt. As it was, Freddie slid feet first into a deep snowbank.

"Oh, look at Freddie, he's planted!" cried Flossie. "Freddie's planted just like a—a bush."

"I'm not a bush," growled her twin. "We—we—went too fast, that's all."

Bert helped his little brother out of the snowdrift and brushed off his clothes.

"We won't go quite so fast after this," he said.

In a little while the Bobbsey twins came to a long hill down which a number of children were coasting.

"Let's go down," said Nan.

"Sure," answered her twin. "But we'll have

to be careful or we'll run into somebody—there are so many sleds."

They took turns coasting, Flossie going down with Nan, and Freddie taking his turn with Bert. Then Nan had a ride alone racing another girl, and Bert went down alone also—racing two boys and coming out ahead by the length of his sled. Nan's race with the other girl was declared a tie.

"But I don't care—Cherry Bonner is a nice girl and I wouldn't want to beat her too badly," said Nan.

"Huh, I'd just as soon beat any boy I know," declared Bert. "It's only in fun, anyway."

After a while the older twins became tired of dragging the sled up the long hill. They turned once again into the level streets and both "sides," as Nan expressed it, took turns at pulling —that is, first the boys pulled and then the girls.

"This is fine," declared Bert when it was his turn to sit on the sled.

"We paid for it, too," added Freddie.

"Paid for it?" questioned Nan.

"Sure. We paid by pulling you first," explained the little fellow.

"Be careful where you are going, Nan!" shouted Bert.

They had come to a corner. Here the snow had been cleared away, leaving a sheet of thin ice on the walk. On this ice the sled spun around, striking a lump of frozen snow, and over it went, sending Bert and Freddie into the street.

As the two Bobbsey boys fell, a car appeared, coming straight toward them.

"Look out!" shrieked Nan.

"Stop!" wailed Flossie. "You'll hit my brothers!"

The man driving the car heard her. He pulled on the steering wheel with all his might. In doing so, he turned the wheel too sharply to the left. The car went into a skid and swerved dangerously close to the boys.

But Bert saw the danger in time and rolled toward the sidewalk, taking Freddie with him. The back wheels of the car missed the two boys by inches. By the time the driver stopped the car and came running back, Bert and Freddie were on their feet, brushing the snow off their clothes.

"Are you boys all right?" the man asked anxiously, his face still white from the fright he had had.

"Oh, yes, sir," Bert spoke up. "Your car never touched us."

"It chased us, but it just couldn't catch us," Freddie added proudly.

"Thank heavens for that," the man said, "because I didn't see you kids and when I did I was going too fast to stop."

After the man went back to his car and drove off, Nan said:

"Oh, Bert, I'm so sorry."

"It wasn't your fault," answered her brother. "That man had no right to drive so fast."

But Nan was still frightened, and to make her forget, Bert piled the two girls and Freddie on the sled in a heap and ran with them a distance of several blocks. He soon had them all shrieking and laughing.

"I'm hungry," announced Freddie suddenly.

"So'm I," said Flossie. "Let's go home."

So homeward went the Bobbsey twins and got there just in time for a good hot supper. And my, how good that supper tasted!

CHAPTER V

BERT'S GHOST

BERT felt relieved to learn that Mr. Ringley did not know who had broken the store window, but he was still fearful that the offense might be laid at his door. He was afraid to trust Danny Rugg, and did not know what the big boy might do about the matter.

"He may say I did it, just to clear himself," thought Bert. "And if Mr. Ringley comes after me, he'll remember me sure."

But his anxiety was forgotten that evening, when some of the neighbors dropped in after dinner. They watched a television show for a while, and almost before Bert and Nan knew it, it was time to go to bed. Freddie and Flossie had already retired, worn out by their play.

But when Bert found himself alone in the small room he occupied, he could not get to sleep. The talk of the grownups downstairs kept him awake at first, and even after they had gone to bed he could not forget the happening of the day.

He could still hear the crash of that glass as the chunk of ice went sailing through Mr. Ringley's store window.

At last he fell into a troubled doze, with the bright light of the moon shining across the quilt at the foot of the bed. But the doze did not last long, and soon some kind of a noise awoke him with a start.

He opened his eyes and his gaze wandered across the moonlit room. Was he dreaming, or was that really a figure in white standing at the foot of his bed? With a shiver he ducked down and covered his head with the blankets.

For two or three minutes he lay quiet, expecting every instant to have something unusual happen. Then, with great caution, he pushed the blankets back and took another look.

There was nothing there!

"But I saw something," he told himself. "I am sure I saw something. What could it have been?"

For over an hour he continued to lie awake, watching and listening. His father was in the next room and he had half a mind to call him, but he was afraid Nan would call him a " 'fraid-cat!"—something he had always despised.

Bert had heard of ghosts and now he thought

of all the ghost stories he could remember. Had the thing in white been a ghost? If so, where had it come from?

After a while he tried to dismiss the thing from his mind, but it was almost morning before he fell asleep again. This time he slept so soundly, however, that he did not wake up until his mother came and shook him.

"Why, Bert, what makes you sleep so soundly this morning?" said Mrs. Bobbsey.

"I—I didn't get to sleep until late," he stammered. And then he added: "Mother, do you believe in ghosts?"

"Why, of course not, Bert. What put that into your head?"

"I—I thought I saw a ghost last night."

"You must have been mistaken. There are no such things as ghosts."

"But I saw something," insisted the boy.

"Where?"

"Right at the foot of the bed. It was all white."

"When was this?"

"Right in the middle of the night."

"Did you see it come in, or go out?"

"No, Mother. When I woke up it was standing there, and when I took a second look at it, it was gone."

"You must have been having a nightmare,

Bert," said Mrs. Bobbsey kindly. "Perhaps you had too many covers over you and were too warm."

"No, it wasn't a nightmare," said the boy.

He had little to say while eating breakfast, but on the way to school he told Nan, while Freddie and Flossie listened with eyes that were almost as big as saucers.

"Oh, Bert, supposing it was a real ghost?" cried Nan, taking a deep breath. "Why, I'd be scared out of my wits—I know I'd be!"

"Mother says there are no ghosts. But I saw something—I am sure of that."

"I don't want to see any ghostses," said Flossie, in a frightened voice.

"Nor I," added Freddie. "Sam told about a ghost once that was as high as a tree an' had six heads, to scare people with. Did your ghost have six heads, Bert?"

"No."

"How many heads did it have?"

"I don't know—one, I guess."

"And was it as high as a tree?" persisted the inquisitive little fellow.

"Oh, it couldn't stand up in the room if it was as high as a tree," burst out Flossie.

"Could if it was a tiny baby tree," argued Freddie.

"It was about as high as that," said Bert, putting out his hand on a level with his shoulder. "I can't say how it looked, only it was white."

"Perhaps it was moonlight," suggested Nan, but at this Bert shook his head. He felt certain it had been more substantial than moonlight.

That day Danny Rugg came to school as usual. When questioned about his absence he said he had had a toothache. When Bert looked at him the big boy merely scowled, and no more words passed between them.

Just outside of Lakeport was a long hill, used during the winter by all the boys and girls for coasting. After school Nan and Bert were allowed to go to this hill, in company with a number of their friends. They were admonished to come home before dark and promised faithfully to do so. It was a much larger hill than the one they had been on before, and there was a bigger crowd.

Among the boys there was a great rivalry as to who could go down the hill the fastest, and who could make his sled go the farthest after the bottom was reached.

"I'll try my sled against yours!" cried Charley Mason to Bert.

"Okay!" returned Bert. "Are you going down alone, or are you going to carry somebody?"

"You must carry me down," insisted Nan.

"Then I'll take Nellie Parks," said Charley.

A few minutes later the two sleds were side by side, with a girl on each. Bert and Charley stood behind.

"Are you ready?" asked Charley.

"Yes."

"Then go!"

Away went both boys, giving each sled a lively shove down the hill. Then each hopped aboard, and took hold of the steering rope.

"A race! A race!" shouted those standing near.

"I think Charley will win!" said some.

"I think Bert will win!" said others.

"Oh, do let's win if we can!" whispered Nan to her twin brother.

"I'll do my best, Nan," muttered Bert as he steered his sled sharply to the left to avoid an abandoned sled.

Down the long hill swept the two sleds, almost side by side. Each was rushing along at a lively rate of speed, and those aboard had to hold on tightly for fear of being jounced off.

"Whoop!" roared Charley. "Clear the track, here we come!"

"Make room for us!" sang out Bert. "We're going to pass you."

The bottom of the hill was almost reached

when Charley's sled began to crawl a bit ahead.

"Oh, Bert, they are going to beat us after all," cried Nan disappointedly.

"I knew we'd beat you," cried Nellie Parks. "Charley's is the best sled on the hill."

"The race isn't over yet," said Bert.

His sled had been running in rather soft snow. Now he turned to where the coasting was better, and in a twinkling his sled shot forward until he was once more beside Charley and Nellie.

"Here we come!" shouted Bert. "Make room, Charley! Make room."

On and on they went, and now the bottom of the hill was reached and they coasted along a level stretch. Charley's sled began to slow up, but Bert's kept right on until he had covered a hundred feet beyond where Charley had slowly come to a stop.

"We've won!" cried Nan excitedly. "Oh, Bert, your sled is a wonder."

"It sure is," he answered with pride. "But it was a close race, wasn't it?"

When they came back to where Charley and Nellie stood, they found Charley rather sulky.

"Nellie is heavier than Nan," said he. "It wasn't a fair race. Let's try it alone next time."

"That's all right with me," answered Bert.

CHAPTER VI

THE COASTING RACE

IT WAS a long walk back to the top of the hill, but Nan and Bert did not mind it as they dragged their sled behind them.

"So you won, did you?" said one of the boys to Bert. "Good for you."

"We are going to try it over again," announced Charley. "Come on."

In the crowd was Danny Rugg, who had a brand-new sled.

"I can beat anybody!" cried Danny boastfully. "This new sled of mine is terrific."

"What a show-off!" whispered Nan to Bert. "If I were you, I wouldn't race with a boy like him."

"I'm going to race with Charley again," answered her twin brother, and took no notice of Danny's challenge.

Bert and Charley lined up their sleds again

45

at the top of the hill, and away they went amid a cheer from their friends.

"I think Charley will win this time," said Nellie.

"And I think that Bert will win," answered Nan loyally.

"Oh, you think your brother is wonderful," sniffed Nellie, with a shrug of her shoulders.

"He is just as good as any boy," said Nan quickly.

Down the hill swept the two sleds, keeping side by side as before. They were but a foot apart, for each owner wished to keep on the hardest part of the slide.

"Keep on your side, Bert Bobbsey!" shouted Charley warningly.

"And you keep on yours, Charley Mason!" returned Bert.

All the others on the hill had stopped coasting to witness the contest, but now with a whoop Danny Rugg leaped on his new sled and came down the hill at top speed.

The two racers had just reached the bottom of the slope when Charley's sled made an unexpected turn and crashed into Bert's, throwing Bert over on his side in the snow.

"What did you do that for?" demanded Bert angrily.

"I—I—didn't do it," stammered Charley. "I guess you turned into me."

"No, I didn't."

Bert arose and began to brush the snow from his clothes. As he did so, he heard a rushing sound behind him and then came a crash as Danny Rugg ran into him. Down he went again and a runner of his sled was completely broken off. Bert was hit in the ankle and badly bruised.

"Why didn't you get out of the way?" roared Danny Rugg roughly. "I yelled loud enough."

"Oh, my ankle!" groaned Bert. For the moment the wrecked sled was completely forgotten.

"I didn't touch your ankle," went on the big boy.

"You did so, Danny—at least your sled did," answered Bert.

"You ran into me in the first place," shouted Charley.

"Oh, Charley, you know better than that." Bert tried to stand, but had to sit down. "Ouch, my ankle!"

"It wasn't my fault," said Danny Rugg, and began to haul his sled away. Charley started to follow.

"Charley, come back here," cried Bert. "I— I guess I can't walk."

Charley hesitated. Then, feeling in his heart

that he was really responsible for running into Bert in the first place, he came back and helped Bert to his feet.

"The sled is broken," said Bert, surveying the wreck dismally.

"That was Danny's fault."

"Well, then, he ought to pay for having it fixed."

"He never pays for anything he breaks, Bert—you know that."

Slowly and painfully Bert dragged himself and his broken sled to the top of the hill. Sharp, hot flashes of pain were shooting through his bruised ankle. Nan ran to meet him.

"Oh, Bert, what is the matter? Are you hurt?" she asked.

"A little—Danny ran into me, and broke my sled."

"It wasn't my fault," blustered the big boy. "You should have gotten out of the way."

"It was your fault, Danny Rugg, and you will have to have my sled fixed," cried Bert.

Throwing down the rope of his own sled, Danny advanced and doubled up his fists as if to fight.

"Don't you talk like that to me," he said in a surly tone. "I don't like it."

Bert's ankle hurt too much for him to continue

the quarrel. He felt himself growing dizzy.

"Let's go home," whispered Nan.

"I'll ride you home if you can't walk," offered Charley, who was now growing alarmed.

In the end Bert had to accept the offer, and home he went, with Charley and Nan pulling him on one sled and dragging the broken sled along behind.

It was all he could do to get into the house. As he hobbled up the steps, Mrs. Bobbsey came to the door very much alarmed. She helped Bert into the living room and took off his shoe and sock. Finding his ankle bruised and swollen, she bathed it with cold water and bound it up.

"You must lie down on the sofa," she said. "Never mind the broken sled. Perhaps Daddy can fix it when he comes home."

Bert detested playing the part of an invalid, but he soon discovered that keeping the ankle quiet made it feel much better than trying to walk around on it.

When Mr. Bobbsey came home he took a look at Bert's ankle and shook his head. "I think we'd better have Dr. Briskett take a look at this," he said to his wife. "It may be a fracture."

Mrs. Bobbsey telephoned Dr. Briskett and the kindly physician came at once. Bert winced when the doctor examined his ankle, but he did not utter a sound. Dr. Briskett removed his glasses and spoke to Mrs. Bobbsey.

"A very bad contusion," he announced. "Luckily it's not broken, but this young man must keep off his feet for a few days."

That night Mr. Bobbsey carried Bert up to bed, and he remained home for three days.

Sam, the handyman, took the broken sled to a carpenter at Mr. Bobbsey's lumber mill and it came back practically as good as new.

"You must not have anything more to do with Danny Rugg," said Mrs. Bobbsey to her son. "He is very rough and disagreeable."

"I'll leave him alone, Mother, if he'll leave me alone," answered Bert.

During those days spent at home, Nan did her best to amuse her brother. As soon as she was out of school she came straight home, and read to him and played games. Nan was also learning to play the piano and she played a number of tunes that he liked to hear. They were so fond of each other that it just did not seem natural for Nan to go out unless her twin brother could go out too.

The first snowstorm had been followed by another, so that in the garden the snow now lay very deep. This was a great delight to Freddie and Flossie, who worked hard to build them-

selves a snow house. They enlisted the services of
Sam, who speedily piled up for them a heap of
snow much higher than their heads.

"Now, children, there's the house," said the
colored man. "All you've got to do is to clear
out the inside." And then he went about his own
work, after starting the hole for them.

Flossie wanted to divide the house into three
rooms, "dining room, kitchen, and bedroom," as
she said, but Freddie objected.

" 'Tisn't big enough," said the little boy.
"Make one big room and call it ev'rything."

"But we haven't got an ev'rything," said Flossie.

"Well, then call it the living room," said Freddie. "When it's done, we can put in a carpet and
two chairs for us to sit on."

It was hard work for such little hands to dig
out the inside of the heap of snow, but they
kept at it, and at last the hole was big enough
for Freddie to crawl into.

"Oh, is this neat!" he cried. "Try it, Flossie!"
And Flossie did try it, and said the house was
going to be perfect.

"Only we must have a window," she added.
"And a curtain just like Mommy's."

They continued to shovel away, and soon
Freddie said he could almost stand up in the

house. He was inside, shoveling out the snow, while his twin sister packed what he threw out onto the outside walls, as Sam had told them to do.

"Where shall I put the window?" asked the little boy.

"On this side," answered Flossie, pointing with her shovel.

At once Freddie began to dig a hole through the side of the pile of snow.

"Be careful, or the house will come down!" cried Flossie. And hardly had she spoken when down came the whole top of the snow pile and poor Freddie was out of sight, completely buried!

CHAPTER VII

THE SNOW HOUSE

"FREDDIE!" Freddie!" shrieked Flossie, when she saw her twin brother disappear. "Come out! Come out!"

But Freddie could not come out, and when, after a few seconds, he did not show himself, she ran toward the kitchen door, screaming at the top of her lungs:

"Oh, Dinah! Dinah! Freddie is buried! Freddie is buried!"

"What's that you say, Flossie?" demanded the cook, coming to the door.

"Freddie is buried. The ceiling of the snow house came down on him!"

"Gracious sakes alive, child!" burst out Dinah, and without waiting to put on a coat she rushed out into the garden. "Give me that shovel quick! He'll be suffocated before you know it."

She began to dig away at the pile of snow, and

presently uncovered one of Freddie's sturdy legs. Then she dropped the shovel and tugged away at the leg and presently brought Freddie to view, just as Mrs. Bobbsey and Nan appeared on the scene.

"What in the world is the matter?" questioned Mrs. Bobbsey in alarm.

"That child went and buried himself alive," responded the colored cook. "The roof of the snow house caved in on him, poor dear! He's most suffocated!"

In the meantime Freddie was gasping for breath. Then he looked at the wreck of the snow house and set up a tremendous wail of dismay.

"Oh, Flossie, it's ruined! The window an' all!"

"Never mind, Freddie dear," said his mother, hugging her little son. "Be thankful that you were not suffocated, as Dinah says."

"Yes, but Flossie and I were makin' an ev'rything house, with a living room, an' a window, an' ev'rything. I didn't want it to fall down." Freddie was still gasping, but now he struggled to the ground. "Want to build it up again," he added.

"I am afraid you'll get into trouble again, Freddie."

"No, I won't, Mommy. Please let us build it up again," pleaded the little fellow.

"I can watch them from the door," suggested Dinah.

"Let me help them, Mother," begged Nan. "Bert is reading a book, so he won't want me for a while."

"Very well, Nan, you stay with them. But all of you be careful," said Mrs. Bobbsey.

After that the building of the snow house was started all over again. The pile of snow was packed down as hard as possible, and Nan made Flossie and Freddie do the outside work while she crept inside, and cut around the ceiling and the window just as the others wanted. It was great fun, and when the snow house was finished it was large enough and strong enough for all of them to enter with safety.

"Tonight I'll pour some water over that house," said Sam. "That will make the snow as hard as ice."

This was done, and the snow house remained in the garden until the warm spring sun melted it right down to the size of a snowball.

Later on that winter Bert built an addition to it, which he called the library, and in this he put a bench and a shelf on which he placed some old magazines and papers.

In the main part Freddie and Flossie placed an old rug and two blocks of wood for chairs, and a small bench for a table. Then, when Flossie grew tired of the house, Freddie turned it into a stable, in which he placed his rocking horse.

Next he brought out his fire engine, and used the place for a firehouse, tying an old dinner bell on a stick, hung over the doorway. Dong, dong! would go the bell, and out he would rush with his little engine and up the garden path, looking for a fire.

"Let us play you are a reg'lar fireman," said Flossie, joining the game. "You must live in the firehouse, and I must be your wife and come to see you with the baby."

She dressed up in a long skirt and paid Freddie a visit, with her best doll in her arms. Freddie pretended to be very glad to see her, and hugged the baby. But a moment later he made the bell ring, and throwing the baby to her, he rushed off again with his engine.

"That wasn't very nice," pouted Flossie. "Dorothy might have fallen in the snow."

"Can't help it," answered Freddie. "A fireman can't stop for anything."

"But—but—he doesn't have to throw his baby away, does he?" questioned Flossie, with wide-open eyes.

"Yes, he does—ev'rything."

"But—but supposing he is—is eating his dinner?"

"He has to throw it away, Flossie. Oh, it's awful hard to be a real fireman."

"Would he have to throw his pie away?"

"Yes."

"Then I wouldn't be a fireman, not for a—a house full of gold!" said Flossie, and marched back into the Bobbsey house with her doll.

Flossie's dolls were five in number. Dorothy was her pride, and had light hair and blue eyes, and three dresses, one a bridal gown. The next was Gertrude, a short doll with black eyes and hair and a traveling dress that was very cute. Then came Lucy, who had lost one arm, and Polly, who had lost both an arm and a leg.

The fifth doll was a clown, dressed in bright yellow with large red polka dots and with enormous shoes. His name was Calico, and he had a huge mouth which extended from ear to ear.

"Calico is always laughing," Flossie would explain to her friends. "He gets into mischief sometimes, and I had to spank him once. It was the time he fell into Dinah's cookie batter. But even then he still smiled, and I was sorry that I had punished him."

The dolls were all kept in a row in a big bureau drawer, and their extra clothes were kept neatly in cardboard boxes in another drawer of the bureau.

With so much snow on the ground it was decided by the boys of that neighborhood to build a snow fort, and this work was undertaken early on the following Saturday morning. Luckily, Bert by that time was able to go out and he did his fair share of the labor, although he was careful not to injure the sore ankle.

The fort was built at the top of a small hill in a large open lot. It was made about twenty feet square and the wall was as high as the boys' heads and over a foot thick. In the middle was gathered a big pile of snow, and into this was stuck a flag-pole from which floated a nice flag loaned by a boy named Ralph Blake.

"Let us divide into two parties of soldiers," said Ralph. "One can defend the fort and the others can attack it."

"Hurrah! Just the thing!" cried Bert. "When shall the battle begin?"

The boys talked it over, and it was decided to have the battle come off after lunch.

The boys went home full of enthusiasm, and soon the news spread that a real soldiers' battle was to take place at the lot.

"Oh, Bert, what fun! I'll come and watch," cried Nan.

"I want to go, too," said Flossie.

"Can't I be a soldier?" asked Freddie. "I can make snowballs, and throw 'em, too."

"No, Freddie, you are too little to be a soldier," answered Bert. "But you can all come and watch if you wish."

After lunch the boys began to gather quickly, until twenty were present. Many girls and a few grown folks were also there. They stood off to one side so no one would be hurt.

"Now, remember," said the father of one of the boys, who volunteered to act as referee. "No ice snowballs and no stones."

"We'll remember, Mr. Potter," cried the young soldiers.

The boys were speedily divided into two parties, one to attack and one to defend the fort. It fell to Bert's lot to be one of the attacking party. Without loss of time each side began to make all the snowballs it could. The boys who remained in the fort kept out of sight behind the walls, while the attacking party moved to the back of the garage at the corner of the big lot.

"Are you all ready?" shouted Mr. Potter presently.

A yell of assent came from the young soldiers on both sides.

"Very well, then. The battle is on!"

Some of the boys had brought horns along,
and now a rousing blast came from behind the
garage and another from the snow fort.

"Come on, fellows, let's capture the fort!"
cried Bert, and led the way, with his arms full of
snowballs.

There was a loud cheer and up the hill rushed
the young soldiers, ready to capture the snow
fort no matter what the cost.

CHAPTER VIII

FUN ON THE ICE

"OH, THE fight is going to start!" cried Nan in high excitement. "See them coming up the hill!"

"Will they shoot?" asked Flossie, just a bit nervously.

"Course they won't shoot," answered Freddie. "Can't shoot snowballs. No gunpowder in snowballs."

The attacking party was still a good distance from the fort when those inside let fly a volley of snowballs. But the snowballs did not reach their mark.

"Now, men, give it to them!" cried Bert, and let fly his first snowball, which landed on the top of the fort's wall.

Soon the air was full of snowballs, flying one way and another. Most of them failed to do any damage, but some went true. Bert received a snowball full in the chest and another in the shoulder. Then he slipped and fell and his snow-balls were crushed under him.

The attacking party got to within fifty feet of the fort, but then the ammunition gave out and they were forced to retreat, which they did in quick order.

"Hurrah! They can't take the fort!" cried those inside the stronghold, and blew their horns more wildly than ever.

But their own ammunition was low and they made other snowballs as quickly as they could, using the pile of snow in the middle of the fort for that purpose.

Back of the garage the attacking party held a consultation.

"I've got a plan," said a boy named Ned Brown. "We'll divide into two parties and one move on the fort from the front and the other from the back. Then, if they attack one party, the other party can sneak in and climb over the fort wall and capture the flag."

"All right, let's do that," said Bert.

Waiting until each boy had a dozen or more snowballs, half the attacking force moved away along a fence until the rear of the fort was gained. Then, with another cheer, all set out for the fort.

It was a grand rush and soon the air was once more filled with snowballs, much to the delight of the spectators, who began to cheer both sides.

"Oh, I hope they get into the fort this time," said Nan.

"I hope they don't," answered another girl, who had a brother in the fort.

The boys inside the fort were having rather a hard time of it. They were close together, and a snowball coming over the walls was almost certain to hit one or another. More than this, the pile of snow around the flag was growing smaller, so that the flag was in great danger of toppling over.

Up the two sides of the hill came the invaders, Bert leading the detachment that was to attack the rear. He was hit again, but did not falter, and a moment later found himself at the very wall.

"Get back there!" roared a boy from the fort and threw a large lump of soft snow directly into his face. But Bert threw the lump back and the defender slipped and fell flat. Then, amid a perfect shower of snowballs, Bert and two other boys fairly tumbled into the fort.

"Defend the flag! Defend the flag!" was the rallying cry of the besieged, and they gathered around the flag. The struggle was now a hand-to-hand one, in which nothing but soft snow was used, and nearly every boy had his face washed.

"Get back there!" roared Danny Rugg, who was close to the flag, but as he spoke two boys shoved him down on his face in the snow. The next moment Bert and another boy of the invading party had the flag and were carrying it away in triumph.

"The fort has fallen!" screamed Nan, and clapped her hands.

"Hurrah!" shouted Freddie. "The—the forters are beaten, aren't they?"

"Yes, Freddie."

A cheer was given for those who had captured the fort. Then some of the boys began to dance on the top of the walls, and down they came, one after another, until the fort was in ruins, and the great contest came to an end.

"It was so exciting!" said Nan to Bert on the way home. "Just like a real battle."

"Only the band didn't play," put in Freddie disappointedly. "Real soldiers have a band. They don't play tin horns."

"Oh, Freddie!" cried Flossie. "They weren't just tin horns. They were Christmas horns."

"It's all the same. I like a band, with a big fat bass drum."

"We'll have the band next time—just for your benefit, Freddie," said Bert.

He was tired out and glad to rest when they got home. More than this, some of the snow had gone down his back, so he had to dry himself by sitting with his back to the living room fireplace.

"Danny Rugg was terribly angry that we captured the fort," he said. "He is looking for the boys who threw him on his face."

"It served him right," replied Nan, remembering the trouble over the broken shoe store window.

The second fall of snow was followed by a spell of steady cold weather and it was not long before the greater part of Lake Metoka was frozen over. As soon as the ice was declared thick enough, nearly all the boys and girls took to skating, so that sledding and snowballing were, for the time being, forgotten.

Both Nan and Bert had new skates, given to them the Christmas before, and each was impatient to go on the ice, but Mrs. Bobbsey held them back until she thought it would be safe.

"You must not go too far from shore," she said. "I understand the ice in the middle of the lake, and at the lower end, is not so firm as it might be."

Freddie and Flossie wanted to watch the skating, and Nan took them to their father's lumberyard. Here there was a small building that served as a yard office directly on the lake front, where they could see much that was going on and still be under the care of an old workman around the place.

Nan could not skate very well, but Bert could get along nicely, and he took hold of his twin sister's hand, and they went gliding over the smooth ice much to their combined delight.

"Someday I am going to learn to do fancy skating," said Bert. "The Dutch Roll, and Spread the Eagle, and all that."

"There is Mr. Gifford," said Nan. "Let's watch him."

The elderly gentleman was a fine skater and had once won a medal for making fancy figures on the ice. They watched him for a long while and so did many of the others present.

"It's beautiful to skate like that," cried Nan, as they skated away. "It's just like knowing how to dance."

"Only better," said Bert, who did not care for dancing at all.

Presently Nan found some girls to skate with and then Bert went off to join the boys. The girls played tag and had great fun, shrieking at the top of their lungs as first one was "it" and then another. It was hard work for Nan to catch the older girls, who could skate better, but easy enough to keep up with those of her own age and experience on the ice.

The boys played tag, too, and "snapped the whip." All the boys would join hands in a long line and then skate off as fast as they could. Then the boy on one end, called the snapper, would stop and pull the others around in a big curve. This would make the boys on the end of the line skate very fast, and sometimes they would go down, and roll over and over on the ice.

Once Bert was at the end and down he went! He skidded along the ice a great distance and bumped smack into a fat man who was skating backwards. Down went the man with a crash that could be heard a long distance off.

"You young rascal!" roared the man, trying to scramble up. "What do you mean by bowling me over like that?"

"Excuse me. I didn't mean to do it," answered Bert, and lost no time getting out of the irate skater's way. The man was very angry and left the ice, grumbling loudly to himself and brushing off his pants.

Down near the lower end of Mr. Bobbsey's lumberyard some older boys were building an iceboat. Bert and Charley Mason watched this work with interest. "Why don't we make an iceboat?" suggested Charley. "I can get an old bed sheet for a sail, if you will get your father to give you the lumber."

"I'll try," answered Bert, and it was agreed that the iceboat should be built during the following week, after school.

CHAPTER IX

CHRISTMAS was not far off now, and the stores of Lakeport had their windows filled with all sorts of nice things for presents. Nan and Bert had gazed into the windows a number of times, and had walked through Taylor's, the one big department store of which the town boasted, and they had told Freddie and Flossie about many of the things they had seen.

"Oh, I want to see them, too!" cried Flossie, and begged her mother to take her along the next time she went downtown.

"I want to go, too," insisted Freddie. "Bert says there are sixteen rocking horses all in a row, with white and black tails. I want to see them."

"I am going tomorrow," answered Mrs. Bobbsey. "You can go with me, after school. It will be better to go now than later on, when the stores are jammed with Christmas shoppers."

The twins were in high glee, and Freddie told Flossie later that he was going to spend the ninety-five cents he had been saving up for several weeks.

"Let us buy Mommy something for Christmas," said Flossie, who had the same amount of money.

"What shall we buy?"

That question was a puzzling one. Flossie thought a fancy pin would be the right thing, while Freddie thought a large box of candy—big enough for the whole family—would be better. At last both consulted Nan.

"Oh, Mother doesn't want a pin," said Nan. "And she is sure to get candy from somebody else, anyway."

"Can't think of anything else she'd like," said Freddie helplessly.

"I'll tell you what to do," suggested Nan. "You buy her a little bottle of cologne, Freddie, and you, Flossie, can buy her a nice handkerchief."

"I'll buy her a big bottle of cologne," said Freddie. "That big!" and he placed his hands about a foot apart.

"And I'll get a real lace handkerchief," added Flossie.

"You'll have to do the best you can," said practical Nan, and all agreed.

When they left home, each child had the money tucked away in a pocket. Sam drove them down to the Lakeport shopping center. The first stop was at Mr. Ringley's shoe store, where Mrs. Bobbsey bought each of the twins a pair of shoes. The broken window glass had long since been replaced by Mr. Ringley, and his show window looked as attractive as ever.

"I heard you had a window broken not long ago," said Mrs. Bobbsey, when paying for the twins' new shoes.

"Yes, two bad boys broke the window," answered the proprietor.

"Who were they?"

"I couldn't find out. But perhaps I'll learn someday, and then I mean to have them arrested," said Mr. Ringley. "The broken glass ruined several pairs of shoes that were in the window." Then he said, "Come again," and turned away to wait on another customer.

Soon they arrived at Taylor's large department store, and Mrs. Bobbsey let Freddie and Flossie take time to look into each of the gaily trimmed windows. One was full of dolls, which made the little girl gasp in wonder and delight.

"Oh, Mommy, what a flock of dolls!" she cried. "Must be 'bout ten millions of them, don't you think so?"

"Hardly that many, Flossie; but there are a good many."

"And, oh, Mommy, what pretty dresses! I wish I had that doll with the pink silk dress and the big lace hat," added the little girl.

"Do you think that is the nicest, Flossie?"

"Oh, yes, Mommy," answered the little girl. "It's just bee-yootiful! Can't we get it and take it home?"

"No, dear, but you had better ask Santa Claus to bring it to you," suggested her mother with a smile.

Some wooden soldiers and building blocks caught Freddie's eye, and for the time being his favorite fire engines were forgotten.

"I want wooden soldiers," he said. "Can set 'em up in a row, with the swordman in front, an' the man with the drum."

"Perhaps Santa Claus will bring you some soldiers in your stocking, Freddie."

"Stocking isn't big enough—want big ones, like that," and he pointed with his chubby hand.

"Well, let us wait and see what Santa Claus can do," said Mrs. Bobbsey.

Inside the store was a candy counter near the doorway, and there was no peace for Mrs. Bobbsey until she had purchased some chocolate drops for Flossie, and a long peppermint cane for Freddie. Then they walked around, down one aisle and up another, admiring the many things which were displayed.

"Bert said they had a escater," said Freddie presently. "Mommy, I want to go on the escater."

"Escater?" repeated Mrs. Bobbsey with a puzzled look. "Why, Freddie, what do you mean?"

"He means the stairs that run up and down," put in Flossie.

"Oh, the escalator," said her mother. "Very well, you shall both ride on the escalator."

It was great fun to ride to the third floor of the store, although the swift way in which the escalator moved made the twins gasp a little.

"Let's go down and come up again," said Freddie. "It's ever so much nicer than climbing the stairs."

"There are a few things I want to buy first," answered his mother.

She had come to buy a rug for the front hallway, and while she was busy in the rug and carpet department, she allowed the twins to look at a number of toys which were located at the other end of the floor.

For a while Freddie and Flossie kept close

together, for there was quite a crowd and they felt a little timid. But then Flossie discovered a counter where all sorts of things for dolls were on sale and she lingered there to look at the dresses, hats, underwear, and shoes and stockings, and chairs, trunks, combs and brushes, and other fascinating articles.

"Oh, my, I must have some of those things for my dolls," she said half aloud. There was a trunk she thought perfectly lovely and it was marked 98 cents. "Not so very much," she thought.

When Freddie got around to where the escalator was, an endless stream of people kept coming up. As he had not seen any down escalator, he concluded that he must go down by way of the stairs if he wanted another ride up.

"I'll get a ride all by myself," he thought.

As quickly as he could, he slipped down first one flight of stairs and then another, to the ground floor of the store. Then he saw more stairs, and soon was in the basement of the department store.

Here was another toy department with a great number of heavy toys, and soon he was looking at a circular railroad track upon which an electric locomotive was speeding. This was certainly a wonderful toy, and Freddie could not take his eyes off it.

In moving around the basement of the store, Freddie grew hopelessly mixed up, and when he started to look for the escalator or the stairs, he walked into a storage room. He was too shy to ask his way out and soon found himself among great rows of boxes and barrels.

Freddie made a few more turns and found himself in another room, filled with empty boxes and cases, some partly filled with straw and excelsior. There was a big wooden door to this room, and while he was inside someone shut the door with a bang and the catch fell into place.

"Oh dear, I wish I was back with Mommy," he thought, and drew a long and exceedingly sober breath. "I don't like it here at all."

Just then a little black kitten came toward him and brushed up against him affectionately. Freddie caught the kitten and sat down for a moment to pet it.

The storeroom was very warm and Freddie now began to feel sleepy. In a few minutes his eyes closed and his head began to nod. Then in a minute more he went sound asleep.

Long before this happened, Mrs. Bobbsey had found Flossie and asked her where Freddie was. The little girl could not tell, and the mother began a diligent search. The section managers in the big store aided her, but it was of no avail.

Freddie could not be found, and soon it was time to close up the establishment for the day. Almost frantic with fear, Mrs. Bobbsey telephoned to her husband, telling him what had happened, and asked him what had best be done.

CHAPTER X

A NEW PET

WHEN Freddie woke up all was very, very dark around him. At first he thought he was at home, and called out for somebody to pull up the blind so that he might see.

But nobody answered him, and all he heard was a strange purring, close to his ear. He put up his hand and touched the little black kitten, which was lying close to his face. He had curled up in the straw and this had proved a comfortable couch upon which to take a nap.

"Oh dear, I'll have to get back to Mommy!" he murmured, remembering where he was, as he struggled up and rubbed his eyes. "What makes it so awful dark? They ought to light the lights. Nobody can buy things when it's so dark as this."

The darkness did not please him, and he was glad to have the black kitten for a companion. With the kitten in his arms he rose to his feet and walked a few steps. Bump! he ran into a big box. Then he went in another direction and stumbled over a barrel.

"Mommy! Mommy!" he cried out. "Mommy, where are you?"

No answer came back to this call, and his own voice sounded so strange to him that he soon stopped. He hugged the kitten tighter than ever.

He was now greatly frightened and it was all he could do to keep back the tears. He knew that it must be night and that the great store must be closed up.

"They have all gone home and left me here alone," he thought. "Oh, what shall I do?"

He knew the night was generally very long and he did not wish to remain in the big, lonely building until morning.

Still hugging the kitten, he felt his way around until he reached the big wooden door. The catch came open with ease, and once more he found himself in that part of the basement used for hardware and large mechanical toys.

The toy engine had stopped, and all was very silent. Only a single light bulb burned overhead, and this cast fantastic shadows which made the little boy think of ghosts and hobgoblins. One mechanical toy had a very large head on it, and this seemed to grin and laugh at him as he looked at it.

"Mommy!" he screamed again. "Oh, Mommy, why don't you come?"

He listened and presently he heard footsteps overhead.

"Who's there?" came the heavy voice of a man.

The voice sounded so harsh in the silent basement that Freddie was afraid to answer. Perhaps the man might be a burglar come to rob the store.

"I say, who's there?" repeated the voice. "Answer me."

There was a minute of silence, and then Freddie heard the footsteps coming slowly down the stairs. The man had a light in one hand and a stick in the other.

Not knowing what else to do, Freddie crouched behind a counter. His heart beat loudly, and he again had visions of burglars who might have entered the big store to rob it. If he was discovered, there was no telling what such burglars might do with him.

"Must have been the cat," murmured the man on the stairs. He reached the basement floor and moved his flashlight over the floor.

"Here, kitty, kitty, kitty!" he called.

"Meow!" came from the black kitten, which was still in Freddie's arms. Then the man looked in that direction.

"Hello!" he exclaimed, staring in amazement. "What are you doing here? Are you alone, sonny?"

"Oh, please, I want my mommy!" cried Freddie.

"You want your mommy?" repeated the man. "Say," he went on suddenly, "are you the kid that got lost this afternoon?"

"I guess I did get lost," answered Freddie. He saw that the man had a kindly face and this made him a bit braver. "I walked around and sat down in there—in the straw—and went to sleep."

"Well, what do you know!" cried the man. "And have you been down here ever since?"

"Yes, sir. But I don't want to stay—I want to go home."

"All right, you shall go. But this beats me!"

"Are you the man who owns the store?" questioned Freddie curiously.

At this the man laughed. "No. Wish I did. I'm the night watchman. And you must be Freddie Bobbsey, Mr. Richard Bobbsey's boy."

"Yes, sir," Freddie replied.

"Well, Freddie, I reckon your daddy will

soon come after you. All of 'em are about crazy, wondering what has become of you."

The night watchman led the way upstairs to the main floor of the department store and Freddie followed, still clutching the black kitten, which seemed well content to remain with him.

"I'll telephone to your daddy," said the watchman, and going into a little office behind the elevators he picked up the telephone and dialed the number of the Bobbsey house.

In the meantime Mrs. Bobbsey and the others of the family were almost frantic with grief and alarm. Mr. Bobbsey had notified the police and the town had been searched thoroughly for some trace of the missing boy.

"Perhaps somebody has kidnaped Freddie!" said Nan, with the tears starting to her eyes.

Mr. Bobbsey had been out a dozen times to police headquarters and to the lake front. A report had come in that a boy about Freddie's age had been seen on the ice early in the evening, and the police thought the little fellow might have wandered in that direction.

When the telephone rang, Mr. Bobbsey had just come in from another fruitless search. Both he and his wife ran to the telephone.

"Hullo!" came over the wire. "Is this Mr. Bobbsey's house?"

"It is," answered Mr. Bobbsey quickly. "What do you want? Have you any news?"

"I've found your little boy, sir," came back the reply. "He is safe and sound with me."

"Thank heavens!" exclaimed Mr. Bobbsey. "And who are you?"

"The night watchman at Taylor's. He went to sleep here, that's all."

At this news the whole family was overjoyed.

"Let me speak to him," said Mrs. Bobbsey eagerly. "Freddie dear, are you all right?" she asked.

"Yes, Mommy," answered Freddie into the telephone. "And I want to come home."

"You shall, dear. Daddy will come for you at once."

"Oh, he's found! He's found!" shrieked Nan. "Aren't you glad, Bert?"

"Of course I am," answered Bert. "But I can't understand how he happened to go to sleep in such a busy store as that."

"He must have walked around until he got tired," replied Nan. "You know Freddie can drop off to sleep very quickly when he gets tired."

After notifying the police that Freddie had been found, Mr. Bobbsey drove around to the department store in his car. The watchman and

Freddie were on the lookout for him, the little boy with the kitten still in his arms.

"Oh, Daddy!" cried Freddie. "I am so glad you have come! I—I don't want to go to sleep here again!"

"The little chap would have been even more frightened if it hadn't been for the kitten," said the watchman. "He wanted to keep the little thing, so I told him he could."

"And I'm going to," said Freddie proudly. "It's just the cutest kitten in the world." And keep the kitten he did. It soon grew up to be a big fat cat and was called Snoop.

By the time home was reached, Freddie was sleepy again. But he speedily woke up when his mother and the others embraced him, and then he had to tell the story of his adventure from beginning to end.

"I don't think I shall take you with me again," said Mrs. Bobbsey. "You have given us all a great fright."

"Oh, Mommy, I won't leave you like that again," cried Freddie quickly. "Didn't have any fun 'tall," he added.

"Oh, it must have been awful," said Flossie. "Didn't you see any—any ghosts?"

"Barrels of them," said Freddie, nodding his

head sleepily. "But they didn't touch me. Guess they were sleepy, just like me."

Soon his little blond head began to nod, and he was put to bed, sound asleep.

And that was the end of Freddie Bobbsey's great adventure.

CHAPTER XI

THE ICEBOAT CRASH

THE building of the iceboat by Bert and Charley Mason interested Nan almost as much as it did the boys, and nearly every afternoon she went down to the lumberyard to see how the work was getting along.

Mr. Bobbsey had given Bert just the right kind of lumber, and had a man at the sawmill saw the sticks and boards to a proper size. He also gave his son some ropes and a pair of iron runners from an old sleigh, so that all Charley had to provide was a good, strong bed sheet for a sail.

The two boys worked with a will, and by Thursday evening had the iceboat completed. They christened the craft the *Ice Bird,* and Bert insisted that his father come and see her.

"You have certainly done very well," said Mr. Bobbsey. "This looks as if you were cut out for a builder, Bert."

"Well, I'd like to build big houses and ships first-rate," answered Bert.

The sail was rigged with the help of an old sailor who lived down by the lake shore, and on Friday afternoon Bert and Charley took a short trip. The *Ice Bird* behaved handsomely, much to the boys' satisfaction.

"She's a dandy!" cried Bert. "How she can whiz before the wind!"

"You must take me out soon," said Nan, when Bert came home.

"I will," answered Bert.

The chance to go out with Bert came sooner than expected. On Monday morning Charley's mother decided to pay a distant relative a visit and asked Charley if he wished to go along. The boy wanted to see his cousins very much and said yes; and thus the iceboat was left in Bert's sole charge.

"I'll take you out Monday afternoon, after school," said Bert to his twin sister.

"Good!" cried Nan. "Let's go as soon as school is out, so we can have some good long rides."

Four o'clock in the afternoon found them at the lake shore. It was a cloudy day with a fair breeze blowing across the lake.

"Now you sit right there," said Bert, as he pointed to a seat in the stern of the boat. "And hold on tight or you'll be thrown overboard."

Nan took the seat indicated, and her twin brother began to hoist the sail of the *Ice Bird*. It ran up easily and caught the wind. The craft began to skim over the surface of the lake like a thing alive.

"Oh, but this is lovely!" cried Nan gleefully. "How fast the boat spins along!"

"I wish there were more iceboats around," answered Bert. "Then we could have a race."

"Oh, it is exciting enough just to sail around," said Nan.

Many other boys and girls wished to ride on the iceboat, and Bert obligingly carried a dozen or more across the lake and back. It was rather hard work tacking against the wind, but the old sailor had taught Bert how to do it, and he got along farily well. When the iceboat got stuck on the shore every once in a while, all the boys and girls got off and helped push the craft along.

"It's almost time for dinner," said Nan, as the whistle at the sawmill blew for five o'clock. "We'll have to go home soon, Bert."

"Oh, let's take one more trip," pleaded her twin brother.

The other boys and girls had gone and they were left alone. To please Bert, Nan consented.

Bert changed their course so that the *Ice Bird* might move down the lake instead of across.

It had grown dark and the stars which might have shone in the sky were hidden by heavy clouds.

"Not too far now, remember," said Nan.

The wind had veered around and was blowing directly down the lake, so, almost before they knew it, the *Ice Bird* was flying along at a tremendous rate of speed. Nan had to hold on tight for fear of falling off.

"Oh, Bert, this is too fast!" she gasped, catching her breath.

"It's just glorious, Nan!" he cried. "Just hold on, it won't hurt you."

"But—how are we to get back?"

Bert had not thought of that, and at the question his face fell a little.

"Oh, we'll get back somehow," he said evasively.

"You had better turn around now."

"Let us go just a little bit farther, Nan," he pleaded.

When at last he started to turn back he found himself unable to do so. The wind was blowing fiercely and the *Ice Bird* swept on before it in spite of all he could do.

"Bert! Bert! Oh, why don't you turn around?"

screamed Nan. She had to scream in order to make herself heard.

"I—I can't," he faltered. "She won't come around."

Nan was very much frightened, and it must be confessed that Bert was frightened, too. He hauled on the sail, pushed the tiller, and at last the *Ice Bird* swung partly around. But instead of returning up the lake the craft headed for the western shore. In a few minutes they struck lumpy ice, snow, and dirt.

The twins were thrown out. The *Ice Bird* was tipped up on one side, the sail flapping in the wind.

Bert picked himself up without difficulty and then went to Nan's aid. She lay deep in the snow, but fortunately was not hurt. Both gazed at the capsized iceboat in dismay.

"Bert, what shall we do now?" asked Nan, after a spell of silence. "We'll never get home at all!"

"Oh, yes, we will," he said, bravely enough, but with a sinking heart. "We've just got to get home."

"But the iceboat is upset, and it's so dark I can't see a thing."

"I think I can right the iceboat. Anyway, I can try."

Doing his best to appear brave, Bert tried to shove the *Ice Bird* over to her original position. But the boat was too heavy for him, and twice the craft fell back, the second time coming close to smashing his toes.

"Look out, or you'll hurt your foot," cried Nan. "Let me help you."

Between them they managed to get the boat right side up. But now the wind was blowing directly from the lake, so to get the *Ice Bird* out on the ice again was beyond them. Every time they shoved the craft out onto the lake, the wind drove her back.

"Oh shucks, I guess we'll have to stay here after all!" sighed Bert at last.

"Not stay here all night, I hope!" gasped Nan. "That would be worse than to stay in the store, as Freddie did."

It was beginning to snow. At first the flakes were few, but soon they came down thicker and thicker, blotting out the already darkened landscape.

"Let's walk home," suggested Nan. "That will be better than staying out here in the snowstorm."

"It's a long walk. If only we had brought our skates." But alas! neither had thought to bring skates, and both pairs were in the office at the lumberyard.

"I don't think we had better walk home over the ice," said Bert, after another pause. "We might get all turned around and lost. Let's walk over to the Hopedale road."

"I wish we had some crullers, or something," said Nan, who was growing hungry. They had each had a cruller on leaving home, but had eaten them before embarking on the iceboat voyage.

"Please don't speak of food, Nan. You make me feel awfully hollow," shouted her twin brother against the roar of the wind. And the way he said this was so comical that it made her laugh in spite of their troubles.

Feeling in better spirits, they left the *Ice Bird* where she lay, and set off through the snow in the direction of the road which ran from Lakeport to the village of Hopedale, six miles away.

"It will take us over an hour to get home," said Nan.

"Yes, and I suppose we'll catch it for being late," grumbled Bert. "Perhaps we won't get any dinner."

"Oh, I know Mother won't scold us after she finds out why we are late, Bert."

They had to cross a pasture and climb a fence before the road was reached. Here they found an old shed and they stood in the shelter of this for a moment, out of the way of the wind and driving snow.

"Listen!" cried Bert, as they were on the point of continuing their journey.

"It's a dog!" answered Nan. "Oh, Bert, he's coming this way. Maybe he'll bite us!"

They listened and could hear the dog plainly. He was barking furiously and coming toward them as fast as he could travel. Soon they made out his black form looming into view through the falling snow.

CHAPTER XII

A BARKING DOG

NAN dearly loved the dogs with which she was well acquainted, but she was very cautious about strange ones, especially if they barked loudly or showed a disposition to bite.

"Bert! Bert! What shall we do?" she gasped as she clung to her twin brother's arm.

Bert hardly knew what to say, for he himself did not like the look of the approaching dog. Glancing around quickly, Bert spied the doorway to the old shed. It was open.

"Let's get into the shed," he said quickly. "Perhaps we can close the door and keep the dog out."

Into the shed sprang Nan and her twin brother. The dog was almost upon them when Bert slammed the door in his face. At once the dog stopped short and began to bark more furiously than ever.

"Do you—you think he can get in at the window?" faltered Nan. She was so frightened she could scarcely speak.

"I don't know. If you'll stand by the door, Nan, I'll try to guard the window."

Nan threw herself against the door and held it as firmly as if a giant were outside trying to force it in. Bert felt around the empty shed and picked up the handle of a broken spade. With this in hand he stalked over to the one little window, which was opposite the door.

"Is there anyone here?" asked Nan. It was so dark she could see next to nothing.

"I don't think so," answered Bert. "This shack is 'most ready to tumble down."

The dog outside was barking still. Once in a while he would stop to catch his breath and then he would continue as loudly as ever. He scratched at the door with his paws, which made Nan shiver from head to feet.

"He is trying to force his way in," she cried.

"If he does, I'll hit him with this," answered Bert bravely, and brandished the spade handle over his head.

He watched the window closely and wondered what they had better do if the dog leaped straight through and attacked them in the dark.

The barking continued for over a quarter of an hour. To Nan and Bert it seemed hours and hours. Then they heard a call from a distance.

"Hey, Tige, what's the matter? Have you spotted a tramp in the shed?"

"Help! Help!" Bert cried. "Call off your dog!"

"A tramp, sure enough," said the man who was coming toward the shed.

"I am not a tramp," answered Bert. "And my sister isn't a tramp, either."

"What's that? You've got your sister with you? Open the door."

"Please, we are afraid of the dog," cried Nan. "He came after us and we ran into the shed for shelter."

"Oh, that's it!" The farmer gave a short laugh. "Well, you needn't be scared! Tige won't hurt you none."

"Are you sure of that?" asked Bert. "He seems to be very fierce."

"I won't let him touch you."

Nan slowly opened the door and followed Bert outside. At a word from the farmer, Tige stopped barking and began to wag his tail.

"That dog wouldn't hurt nobody, unless he was attacked, or unless a person tried to get into my house," said Farmer Sandborn. "He's a very nice fellow, he is, and likes boys and gals first-rate. Don't you, Tige?" The dog wagged his tail harder than ever, as if he understood every word.

"I—I was so frightened," said Nan.

"May I ask what you kids are doin' on the road all alone and in this snowstorm?"

"We are going home," answered Bert. He explained how they had been iceboating and what had happened on the lake.

"Well, what do you know about that!" cried Farmer Sandborn. "So the boat up an' run away with you, did she? Contrary critter, eh?" And he began to laugh. "Who are you?"

"I am Bert Bobbsey and this is my twin sister Nan."

"Oh, yes, I know now. You're one pair o' the Bobbsey twins, as they call 'em over to Lakeport. I've heard Sary speak o' you. Sary's my wife." The farmer rubbed his chin thoughtfully. "You can't tramp home in this storm."

"Oh, we must get home," said Nan. "What will Mother say? She will think we are killed, or drowned, or something—and she isn't over the scare she got when Freddie was lost."

"I'll drive you back to town in my car," said Farmer Sandborn. "I was going to town for some groceries tomorrow morning, but I might just as well go now, while the roads are still open. They'll all be closed up by daylight, if this storm keeps up."

He led the way down the road to his house and they were glad enough to follow. By Nan's side walked Tige and he licked her hand, just to show that he wanted to make friends with her.

"I guess you're a good dog after all," said she, patting his head. "But you did give me such a scare!"

Both the twins were very cold and glad to warm themselves by the kitchen fire before starting for home. The farmer's wife wanted to give them supper, but this they declined.

"We'll get supper at home," said Nan. "But I thank you just the same."

"So do I," added her twin.

"Well, you young ones must be hungry—bein' out in the cold," declared the farmer's wife. "Maybe you'd like to have a cooky, anyway."

Nan was about to refuse politely, when she caught Bert's eye. He was nodding hopefully. Actually, the poor Bobbsey boy thought he had never in his life been so hungry as he was right now.

"Well, I don't know—" Nan began.

"Sure, you'll have a cooky," said Mrs. Sandborn. "Young folks always like my cookies. See here!"

She brought from the pantry a big stone jar. Taking off the cover, she showed about two dozen big cookies, each liberally sprinkled with powdered sugar.

"I make 'em for my grandchildren," she explained. "I have five of 'em—three girls an' two boys. They're always as hungry as bears, 'specially in cold weather. So I keep the cookies handy. Here, try this."

She handed a big cooky to Nan and an equally big one to Bert. The twins bit into them hungrily and found them fully as good as those baked by Dinah.

"They're awfully good," said Bert.

"Indeed they are," added Nan. "Thank you. And it's very kind of Mr. Sandborn to drive us home, too."

"Oh, it's nothin'," said the woman. "He'd have to go to town tomorrow if he didn't tonight. An' maybe travelin' is better today."

"Well, it won't be so good tomorrow, if it snows some more," said Bert.

"Land sakes alive, I do wish it would stop snowin'. I believe snow gives me rheumatism."

"That's too bad," said Nan sympathetically.

"I'm sure I wouldn't want to get rheumatism," said Bert.

"Young folks don't get it often. That's a left-handed blessin' old folks get."

Soon Farmer Sandborn drove around to the door in his car and in they piled.

"It's nice riding through the snow," declared Bert. And yet they did not enjoy it very much, for fear of what would happen to them when they got home.

"Where in the world have you been?" exclaimed Mrs. Bobbsey as she ran to the door to let them in. "We have been looking all over for you. Your father was afraid you had gone through the ice and been drowned in the lake."

A late supper was waiting for them, and sitting down to satisfy their hunger, they told their story, to which all of the others listened with much interest.

"You can be thankful you weren't blown clear to the other end of the lake," said Mr. Bobbsey. "I think after this you had better leave iceboating alone."

"I know I shall!" declared Nan.

"Oh, I'll be more careful, Dad, after this," pleaded Bert. "You know I promised to go out again with Charley."

"Well, then, don't go when the wind is strong." And Bert promised.

"I'm so glad the dog didn't bite you," said little Flossie. "You might have got hy—hydropics."

"Flossie means hydrophobics," put in Freddie. "No such thing as hydropics, is there, Bert?"

"Oh, Freddie, you mean hydrophobia!" burst out Nan with a laugh.

"No, I mean hydrophobics," insisted the little fellow. "That's what Dinah calls them, anyway."

After the adventure in the iceboat, matters ran smoothly with the Bobbsey twins for quite a while. There was a great deal of snow and several times it was too cold to play outdoors very long, after school. During those days all the children had great fun in the attic, where there was a large storeroom filled with all sorts of things.

"Let's play theater," said Nan who had been to several plays both in Lakeport and while visiting.

"All right," said Bert, falling in with the plan at once. "Let's play Rip Van Winkle. I can be Rip and you can be the loving wife, and Flossie and Freddie can be the children."

Across the storeroom a rope was placed and on this they hung a sliding curtain, made out of a discarded blanket. Then at one side they arranged chairs, and Nan and Flossie brought out their dolls to be the audience.

"They won't clap their hands very much,"

said Bert. "But then they won't make any disturbance either."

The performance was a great success. It was their own version of Rip Van Winkle, and Bert as old Rip did many funny things which caused Freddie and Flossie to roar with laughter.

Nan as the loving wife recited a piece "Doughnuts and Daisies," pretending to be working around the kitchen in the meantime. The climax was reached when Bert tried to imitate a thunderstorm in the mountains and pulled over a big trunk full of old clothes and some window screens standing in a corner.

The show broke up in a hurry. When Mrs. Bobbsey appeared on the scene, wanting to know what the noise meant, all the actors and the doll audience were out of sight.

After seeing that no serious damage had been done, Mrs. Bobbsey went below again. In a few seconds Bert and Nan came out from their hiding place. Bert called to Freddie and Flossie.

"All stagehands come out from wherever you are."

Quickly the trunk and the screens were put in their proper places, and the four Bobbseys, working together, soon had the attic in order again.

CHAPTER XIII

NAN BAKES A CAKE

"LET'S!" cried Nan.

"Yes, let's!" echoed Flossie.

"I want to help too," put in Freddie. "Want to make a cake all by my own self."

"Freddie can make a little cake while we make a big one," said Bert.

It was on an afternoon just a week before Christmas and Mrs. Bobbsey had gone out to do some shopping. Dinah was also away, on a visit to some relatives, so the children had the house all to themselves.

It was Bert who spoke about cake baking first. Queer that a boy should think of it, wasn't it? But Bert was very fond of cake, and did quite some grumbling when none was to be had.

"It ought to be easy to make a nice big plain cake," said Bert. "I've seen Dinah do it lots of times. She just mixes up her eggs and milk and butter, and sifts in the flour, and there you are."

"Much you know about it!" declared Nan. "If it isn't put together just right, it will be as heavy as lead."

"We might take the recipe out of Mother's cookbook," went on Bert; and then the cry went up with which I have opened this chapter.

The twins were soon in the kitchen, which Dinah had left spotlessly clean and in perfect order.

"We mustn't make a mess," warned Nan. "If we do, Dinah will never forgive us."

"As if we couldn't clean it up again," said Bert loftily.

Over the kitchen table they spread some old newspapers, and then Nan brought forth the big bowl in which her mother or the cook usually mixed the cake batter.

"Bert, you get the milk and sugar," said Nan, and began to roll up her sleeves. "Flossie, you can get the butter."

She would have told Freddie to get something, too—just to start them all to work—but Freddie was out of sight.

He had gone into the pantry, where the flour barrel stood. He did not know that Nan intended to use the prepared cake flour, which was on the shelf. The door worked on a spring, so it had closed behind him, shutting him out of sight of the others.

Taking off the cover of the barrel, Freddie looked inside. The barrel was almost empty, only a few inches of flour remaining at the bottom. There was a flour scoop in the barrel, but he could reach neither this nor the flour itself.

"I'll have to stand on the bench," he said to himself and pulled the bench into position. Then he stood on it and bent down into the barrel as far as possible.

The others were working in the kitchen when they heard a strange *thump* and then a spluttering yell.

"It's Freddie," said Nan. "Bert, go and see what he is doing in the pantry."

Bert ran to the pantry door and pulled it open. A strange sight met his gaze. Out of the top of the barrel stuck Freddie's legs, with a cloud of flour dust rising around them. From the bottom of the barrel came a succession of coughs, sneezes, and yells for help.

"Freddie has fallen into the flour barrel!" Bert cried, and lost no time in catching his brother by the feet and pulling him out.

It was hard work and in the midst of it the

flour barrel fell over on its side, scattering the fine white flour all over Dinah's clean pantry floor.

"Oh! Oh! Oh!" gasped Freddie as soon as he could catch his breath. "Oh, my! Oh, my!"

"Oh, Freddie, why did you go into the barrel?" exclaimed Nan, wiping her hands and running to him. "Did you ever see such a sight?"

Freddie was digging at the flour in his eyes. He was white from head to feet, and coughing and spluttering.

"Wait, I'll get the whisk broom," said Bert, and ran for it.

"Brush off his hair first, and then I'll wipe his face," cried Nan.

"Here's the dishcloth," put in little Flossie, and catching it up, wringing wet, she began to wipe off Freddie's face before anybody could stop her.

"Flossie! You mustn't do that!" said Bert. "Don't you see you are making paste of the flour?"

The wet flour speedily became a dough on Freddie's face and neck, and he yelled louder than ever. The dishcloth was put away, and regardless of her own clean clothes, Flossie began to scrape the dough off, until both Nan and Bert made her stop.

"I'll dust him good first," said Bert, and began such a vigorous use of the whisk broom that everybody began to sneeze.

"Oh, Bert, not so hard!" said Nan, and ran to open the back door. "Bring him here."

Poor Freddie had a lump of dough in his left ear and was trying in vain to get it out with one hand while rubbing his eyes with the other. Nan brushed his face gently, and even wiped the end of his tongue, and got the dough out of his ear. In the meantime Flossie started to set the flour barrel up once more.

"Don't touch the barrel, Flossie!" called Bert. "You keep away, or you'll be as messy as Freddie."

It was very hard work to get Freddie's clothes even half clean, and some of the flour refused to budge from his hair. By the time he was made half presentable once more, the kitchen was in a mess from end to end.

"What were you doing near the flour barrel?" asked Nan.

"Going to get flour for the cake."

"But we don't want that kind of flour, Freddie. We want this," and she brought out the package of prepared flour.

"Dinah uses this," answered the little boy.

"Yes, sometimes. But we are going to use cake

flour. You had better sit down and watch Bert and me work, and you, Flossie, had better do the same."

"No chairs to sit down on," said Freddie, after a look around. "All covered with flour."

"Goodness, we forgot to dust the chairs," answered Nan. "Bert, will you clean them?"

Bert did so, and Freddie and Flossie sat down to watch the process of cake making, being assured that they would have the first slices if the cake were a success.

Nan had watched cake making many times, so she knew exactly how to go to work. Bert was a good helper, and soon the batter was ready for the oven. The oven had been lighted, and now Nan put the batter in the cake tin.

The children waited impatiently while the cake was baking. Nan gave Freddie another brushing, and Bert cleaned up the pantry and the kitchen floor. The flour had made a dreadful mess and the cleaning process was only half successful.

" 'Most time for that cake to be done, isn't it?" questioned Bert, after a quarter of an hour had passed.

"Not quite," answered Nan.

"I don't want to wait all day," complained Freddie.

"Freddie, you keep still or you shan't have any."

At this threat the little boy became very much subdued.

"Come on, we'll sing a song—then maybe the cake will be done," cried Bert.

He and Nan started one of their school songs. Then Bert began to dance around the kitchen with Freddie and Flossie.

"Now, I'm sure it must be done," said Flossie after the romping had come to an end.

"Just a few minutes more," said Nan.

Presently she opened the oven door and tried the cake by sticking a broom whisk into it. The flour was still just a bit sticky and she left the cake in a little longer.

When it came out, it certainly looked very nice. The top was a golden brown and had risen beautifully. The cake was about a foot in diameter and Nan was justly proud of it.

"Wish you had put raisins in it," said Freddie. "Raisins are awful good."

"No, I like plain cake the best," said Bert.

"I like choc'late," said Flossie.

"And I like layer cake, with currant jelly in between," said Nan. "But I didn't dare to open any jelly without asking Mother."

"Let's surprise her with the cake," said Bert.

"Want it now," protested Freddie. "Don't want to wait 't all!"

But he was persuaded to wait, and the cake was hidden away in the dining-room closet until the hour for the evening meal.

When Dinah came home she noticed the flour around the kitchen. Nan told her about the accident and Dinah said she would keep their secret.

"Everything will be all right, honey," said the colored cook. "But I'd 'a' known you been a bakin' anyway—I can smell it in the air."

When they sat down to the evening meal, the children produced the cake in great triumph.

"Oh, Nan, a cake!" cried Mrs. Bobbsey. "How nice it looks!"

"We've got some real housekeepers around here," said Mr. Bobbsey. "I'll have to try that cake by all means."

When the cake was cut, the whole family ate liberally of it. They declared it could not be better. Even Dinah was tickled.

"Couldn't do no better myself," she insisted. "Someday Dinah will be cut out of a job—with Miss Nan a-doin' all the bakin'."

"No, Dinah, you shall stay even if I do the baking," answered Nan; and went to bed that night feeling very happy.

CHAPTER XIV

CHRISTMAS

AS CHRISTMASTIME drew close, all the Bobbsey children tried to guess what Santa Claus would bring them and what they would receive from their out-of-town relatives.

Freddie and Flossie had made out long lists of the things they hoped to get. Freddie wished a fireman's suit and a real trumpet, a railroad track with a locomotive that could go, and some building blocks and picture books.

Flossie craved more dolls and dolls' dresses, a real trunk with a lock, fancy slippers, a pair of rubber boots, and some big card games.

"All I want is an angora sweater," said Nan, not once but many times. "A beautiful pink one, just like Mother's."

"And all I want is some good adventure books, some games, a new pocketknife, a catcher's mitt, and some money," said Bert.

"Well! You don't want much, Bert," cried Nan. "How much money—a thousand dollars?"

"I want money, too," piped up Freddie. "Want to start a bank account just like Daddy's."

By putting a little of their allowance away each week, Bert and Nan had accumulated six dollars and ten cents between them, while Freddie and Flossie had each saved ninety-five cents. There was a great deal of planning among the twins, and all put their money together, to buy Mother and Daddy and Dinah and Sam some Christmas presents.

Freddie and Flossie had not yet purchased the cologne and handkerchief Nan had suggested, and now it was decided to get Mr. Bobbsey a new necktie, Mrs. Bobbsey a Christmas plant, Dinah a fancy apron, and Sam a pair of gloves. Nan and Bert made the purchases which, after being duly inspected by all, were hidden away in the attic storeroom.

As the time until Christmas grew shorter, Flossie and Freddie became very anxious, wanting to know if Santa Claus would be sure to come. Flossie inspected the chimney several times.

"It's a dreadfully small place and very dirty,"

she said. "I am afraid Santa Claus won't be able
to get down with a very big load. And some of his
things will get all broken up."

"Santa Claus can spirit himself wherever he
wants to, dear," said Mrs. Bobbsey with a quiet
smile.

"What do you mean by spirit himself,
Mommy?"

Before Mrs. Bobbsey could answer Flossie's
question, she was called to the telephone.

"Does Mommy mean a ghost?" Flossie asked
Nan.

"No, Flossie; she means that part of a person
that lives but can't be seen."

"Oh, I know," cried the child, brightening.
"It's just like when a person is good. Then they
say it's the *spirit* of goodness within him. I guess
Mommy means it's the good spirit of Santa Claus
that can't be seen."

Freddie and Flossie grew more and more impatient each day. Many times they whispered
together about the Christmas presents and once
Bert caught them looking over the things that
had been bought.

"You mustn't do that," said the older Bobbsey
boy. "Somebody might see you and that would
spoil everything."

"Can't see us," said Freddie. "We came up all alone."

"Mommy's gone to the store," chimed in his twin sister.

"But Dinah or Sam might come up here."

"Sam went out for Daddy."

"An' Dinah is in the cellar bringing up the glasses of cranberry jelly."

Just then the children heard a noise below, followed by the slamming of a door.

"It's Sam coming in!" cried Bert.

Then came voices and presently they heard Dinah call out:

"Children! Where are you?"

"Oh, she'll find us, sure!" exclaimed Bert. "Put those presents away, quick!"

He and the others caught up the presents. But the box containing the gloves for Sam fell from Freddie's hands out of sight under an old stand.

"Oh, Sam's gloves are lost!" wailed Freddie.

"Quick, get them," said Bert hoarsely. "We're coming, Dinah!" he called down the stairs.

Freddie made a dive under the stand and came up with his nose full of dust but with the precious box in his chubby hands. Quickly the gloves were put away. Then the children trooped down the stairs.

"Here we are, Dinah," said Bert. "What do you want of us?"

"Wanted to know if you was in the house," said the cook.

"Oh," returned Bert, and winked at the smaller twins—and Freddie tried to wink in return, while Flossie giggled.

On the day before Christmas the living-room door was closed and locked, so that none of the children might enter the room. Freddie was very anxious to look through the keyhole, but Bert told him that wouldn't be fair, so he stayed away.

"We are to hang up our stockings on the dining-room mantel tonight," said Nan. "And Mother says we must go to bed early, too."

"That's to give Santa Claus a chance to get around," said Freddie. "Daddy said so. He said Santa Claus had his hands more than full, with so many boys and girls all over the world to take care of."

"Santa Claus must be a twin, just like you and me," said Flossie. "Maybe he's a twin a hundred times over."

At this Freddie roared. "What a funny twin that would be—with each one having the same name!"

The stockings were hung up with great care, and Freddie and Flossie made up their minds to stay awake and watch Santa Claus at his work.

"Won't say a word when he comes," said the little boy. "Just peek out at him from under the covers."

But alas! long before Santa Claus paid his visit that Christmas Eve, both Freddie and Flossie were in dreamland, and so were Bert and Nan.

It was Flossie who was the first to awake in the morning. For a moment, after she opened her eyes and sat up, she could not remember why she had awakened this early. But it was for some reason, she was sure of that.

"Merry Christmas!" she burst out, all at once, and the cry awoke Freddie.

"Merry Christmas, ev'rybody!" the little boy roared, at the top of his lungs.

The last call awoke Nan and Bert, and before long all were scrambling out to see what the stockings might contain.

"Oh, I've got a doll!" shrieked Flossie, and brought forth a darling blue-eyed baby doll.

"I have a jumping jack!" came from Freddie, and he began to work the toy up and down in a most comical fashion.

There was some small gift for everybody and several apples and oranges besides, and quantities of nuts and hard candies in the stockings.

"We must get the presents for the others," whispered Nan to Bert and the smaller twins, and soon all were dressed and bringing the things down from the storeroom.

It was a happy party that gathered in the dining room. "Merry Christmas!" said everybody to everybody else, and then Mr. Bobbsey threw open the living-room doors.

There, beside the fireplace, stood a beautiful Christmas tree, loaded down with pretty ornaments, candy canes, silver tinsel, and many pretty-colored lights. Around the bottom of the tree were heaps of brightly wrapped presents with little tags on them telling whom they were meant for.

"Oh, there's the dolly with the pink silk dress!" screamed Flossie, and caught the big doll up in her arms and kissed it.

Soon all the Bobbsey children were on their hands and knees untieing their presents.

"And look at my fireman's suit!" roared Freddie, and then, seeing a trumpet, he took it up and bellowed:

"Bring up the engine! Play away lively there!" just like a real fireman.

Bert had his books and a catcher's mitt, and under them was hidden a new bankbook, showing that there had been deposited to his credit ten dollars in the Lakeport Savings Bank. Nan had a similar bankbook, and of these the twins were very, very proud. Bert felt as if he was truly getting to be quite a businessman.

"Oh! Oh!" cried Nan, as she opened a big box that was at the bottom of her pile of presents; and then the tears of joy stood in her eyes as she brought forth the hoped-for angora sweater. It was beautiful, and so soft that she could not resist brushing it against her cheek over and over again.

"Oh, Mother, I think it is too lovely for anything!" she said, rushing up and kissing her mother. "I'm sure no girl ever had such a beautiful sweater before!"

"You must try and keep it nice, Nan," answered her mother.

"I'll take the very best care of it," said Nan, and she really did.

"And now we have something for you, too," said Bert, and brought out the various articles.

Flossie gave their mother her present, and Freddie gave his father the necktie. Then Nan gave Dinah the fancy apron, and Bert handed Sam the new gloves.

"Well, this is truly a surprise!" cried Mr. Bobbsey, as he inspected the necktie. "It is just what I need."

"And this poinsettia is beautiful," said Mrs. Bobbsey, admiring her Christmas plant. "It will bloom a long while, I'm sure."

Dinah was tickled over the apron and Sam with his gloves.

"You children are the sweetest in the world," said the cook.

"These gloves are the very thing I needed to keep my hands warm!" exclaimed Sam.

It was fully an hour before the children felt like sitting down to breakfast. All were almost too excited to eat. Before they began, Mr. Bobbsey brought out the family Bible and read the wonderful story of Christ's birth to them.

After breakfast, the Bobbsey twins decided to go visiting. They wanted to show off their new presents and were anxious to see what their friends had received. It was truly a happy time. Then the children went coasting until it was time for Christmas dinner.

"The expressman is coming!" cried Bert, who had kept an eye on the house. And sure enough, the expressman was stopping in front of the Bobbsey home.

The man jumped off the truck, carrying two boxes. The children dashed up to find that one was from their Uncle Daniel Bobbsey, who lived at Meadow Brook, and the other from their Uncle William Minturn, who lived at Ocean Cliff.

"More presents!" cried Nan, and she was right. Their uncles and aunts had sent each twin something; and the children insisted that each package be opened immediately.

"Oh, Christmas is just the best day in the whole year," said Bert that evening, after the eventful day was over.

"Wish Christmas would come ev'ry week," said Freddie. "Wouldn't it be wonderful?"

"If it did, I'm afraid the presents wouldn't reach," said Mrs. Bobbsey laughing, and hustled the sleepy little twins off to bed.

CHAPTER XV

THE CHILDREN'S PARTY

THE little black kitten that Freddie had brought home from Taylor's department store was a great friend of everybody in the Bobbsey house, and they all loved the little animal very much.

At first Freddie had started to call the kitten Blackie. Flossie said that wasn't a very " 'ristocratic" name at all.

"I'll tell you what," said Bert jokingly, "let's call him Snoop." And in spite of all efforts to make the name something else, Snoop the cat remained from that time on.

He grew very fat and just a trifle lazy. Nevertheless he learned to do several tricks. He could sit up in a corner on his hind legs, and shake hands, and when told to do so would jump through one's arms, even if the arms were held quite high up from the floor.

Snoop had one comical trick that always made

both Flossie and Freddie laugh. There were two shiny faucets in the sink, and Snoop loved to sit on the edge of the sink and play with the drops as they fell from the bottom of the faucets. He would watch until a drop was just falling, then reach out with his paw and give it a claw just as if he were reaching for a mouse.

Another trick which he had, though this Mrs. Bobbsey did not think so nice, was to curl himself on the pillow of one of the beds and go sound asleep. Whenever he heard Mrs. Bobbsey coming upstairs, he would fly off the bed and sneak down the back stairs, so that she rarely caught him.

Snoop was a very clean cat and was continually washing his face and his ears. Around his neck Flossie placed a blue ribbon, and it was amusing to see Snoop try to wash it off. But after a while, having spoiled several ribbons, he found they would not wash off, and so he let them alone, and in the end appeared very proud of them.

One day, not long after Christmas, Snoop could not be found anywhere.

"Snoop! Snoop!" called Freddie, upstairs and down.

The kitten did not answer, nor did he show himself. Then Flossie called him and made a search but was equally unsuccessful.

"Perhaps somebody has stolen him," said Freddie, tears coming to his eyes.

"Nobody has been here to steal that kitten," answered Dinah. "He's just sneaked off, that's all."

All the children had been invited to a party that afternoon, and Nan was going to wear her new angora sweater. After having brushed her hair, Nan put on a blue skirt and went to the closet in which her pink sweater was kept in a box.

"Well, what do you think of that!" she exclaimed. "Oh, Snoop, how could you do it!"

For there, curled up on the sweater, was the kitten, purring as contentedly as could be. Never before had he found a bed so soft or so much to his liking. But Nan made him rouse up in a hurry, and after that when she closed the closet door, she made quite sure that the cover of the box was on tight and that Snoop was not inside the closet.

The party to be held that afternoon was at the home of Grace Lavine, the little girl who had fainted from so much rope jumping. Grace had recovered from that attack, and was now quite certain that when her mother asked her not to do something, it was always for her own good.

"I guess Mother really does know best," she

admitted to Nan. "I didn't think so then, but I do now."

The party was a grand affair and over thirty children were present, all dressed in their best. They played all sorts of games such as musical chairs and others you know, and then some new games which the big boys and girls introduced.

One game was called Hunt the Beans. A handful of dried beans was hidden all over the rooms, in out-of-the-way corners, behind the piano, and in vases. At the signal every girl and boy started to pick up as many beans as could be found. The search lasted just five minutes, and at the end of that time the one having the most beans won the prize.

"Now let us play Three-Word Letters," said Nan. And then she explained the game. "I will call out a letter and you must try to think of a sentence of three words, each word starting with that letter. Now then, are you ready?"

"Yes! Yes!" the girls and boys cried.

"B," said Nan.

There was a second of silence.

"Boston Baked Beans!" shouted Charley Mason.

"That is right, Charley. Now it is your turn to give a letter."

"F," said Charley.

"Five Fat Fairies!" cried Nellie Parks.

"Four Fresh Fish," added another of the girls.

"Nellie has it," said Charley. "But I never heard of fat fairies, did you?"

"Of course," Nan replied. "Daddy calls Flossie his Fat Fairy." That made everybody laugh.

"My letter is M," said Nellie, after a pause.

"More Minced Mushrooms," said Bert.

"More Mean Men," said another boy.

"Mind My Mule," said one of the girls.

"Oh, Helen, I didn't know you had a mule," cried Flossie, and this caused a wild shriek of laughter.

"Bert must love mushrooms," said Nellie.

"I do," said Bert, "if they are in a sauce." And then the game went on, until somebody suggested something else.

At seven o'clock a supper was served. There were two tables, with the little girls and boys at one, and the big girls and boys at the other. Each was decked out with flowers and with colored streamers, which ran down from the ceiling light to each corner of both tables.

There was a load of good things to eat and drink—chicken sandwiches and cake, with cups of sweet chocolate, or lemonade, and then more cake and ice cream, and fruit, nuts, and candy.

The ice cream was made up in various fancy

forms, and Freddie got a fireman with a trumpet under his arm, and Nan a little Dutch girl with wooden shoes. Bert was served with an automobile, and Flossie cried with delight when she received a brown-and-white cow that looked as natural as life.

All of the forms were so pleasing that the children did not care to eat them until the heat in the warm dining room made them begin to melt away.

"I'm going to tell Dinah about the ice-cream cow," said Flossie. "Perhaps she can make them." But when appealed to later, Dinah said they were beyond her, and must be purchased from the professional ice-cream maker, who had the necessary forms.

There were dishes full of party snappers on the tables, and soon the snappers were snapping at a lively rate among the big girls and boys, although the younger children were rather afraid of them. Each snapper had a fortune paper in it and some sort of fancy article made of paper. Bert got an apron, which he promptly pinned on, much to the amusement of the girls. Nan drew an admiral's hat and put it on, and this caused another laugh.

There were all sorts of caps, hats, and aprons, and one big snapper, which went to Flossie, had a complete dress in it, of pink and white paper. Another had some artificial flowers, and still another a tiny bottle of perfume.

While the supper was going on, Mr. Lavine had darkened the living room. As soon as the young people were through eating they were treated to a home movie by Grace's father, assisted by Bert. There were all sorts of scenes, including some which were very funny and made the boys and girls shriek with laughter.

One was a boy on a donkey, and another showed two fat men trying to climb over a fence. Then came a number of pictures taken by Mr. Lavine himself with his movie camera, showing scenes in and around Lakeport.

There were the lake steamer, and the main street, and one was a picture of the girls and boys rushing out of school at lunchtime. The last was voted the best of all, and many of the children present were able to pick themselves out of this picture.

After the movies were over, one of the older girls sat down at the piano and played. By this time some of the parents began drifting in, and they called for some singing, and all joined in half a dozen songs that were familiar to them.

In a little while the young folks ran off for

their coats and hats, and thanked their host and hostess and bade each other good night.

"Wasn't it fun?" said Nan, on the way home. "I never had such a good time before."

"Didn't last half long enough," said Freddie. "Want it to last longer next time."

"I wanted my cow to last longer," said Flossie. "Oh, if only I could have kept it from melting!"

CHAPTER XVI

A GRAND SLEIGH RIDE

FOR a long while all the Bobbsey children had been begging their parents for an old-fashioned sleigh ride into the country.

"The winter will be gone soon, Daddy," said Nan. "Won't you take us before the snow is all gone?"

"You may as well take them, Richard," said Mrs. Bobbsey.

"Well, if I do, Mary, you must go along," answered Mr. Bobbsey, and so it was arranged that they should take a ride to Dalton on the following Saturday, weather permitting.

You may well suppose that all the twins were very anxious about the weather after that, for Mr. Bobbsey said they would not go if it rained or if it snowed very hard.

"What does it say in the newspapers?" asked Freddie. "They always know what the weather is going to be."

"Not so far ahead as that," answered his brother.

But Friday evening the paper said cold and clear, and sure enough, on Saturday morning it was as nice as anyone could wish. From behind masses of thin clouds the sun peeped shyly, lighting up the snow until it shone like huge beds of diamonds.

The road to Dalton was a back road which had not been scraped as clear of snow as the main-traveled roads. Mr. Bobbsey had found an old sleigh in a shed at the lumberyard, and had hired for the day a big gray horse from a near-by riding stable. He also had arranged for the family to stop for dinner with friends in Dalton.

By half-past nine the old-fashioned sleigh was at the door, with Sam on the front seat, driving. Into the sleigh piled the four children, and Mr. and Mrs. Bobbsey followed.

"Want to sit by Sam and help drive," Freddie said firmly, and he was lifted over to the desired position. Then off they went, with a crack of the whip and jingling of sleigh bells that could be heard a long distance.

"Oh, isn't this just too wonderful for anything!" exclaimed Nan, who sat at one side of the seat, with her mother on the other and Flossie between them. "I wish we could sleigh ride all the time. It's ever so much more fun than an automobile."

"See me drive!" cried Freddie. He held the very end of the reins, the part dangling from Sam's hands.

"Well, Freddie, don't let the horse run away," said Mr. Bobbsey with a laugh.

"I won't," answered the little fellow soberly. "If he tries to run away, I'll whip him good."

"You'll never stop a horse that way," said Bert. "You want to talk gently to him."

On and on they went, over the smooth snow. The horse was fresh and full of spirit, and mile after mile was covered with a speed that pleased all the twins very much.

They passed several automobiles parked along the road, and the children set up a merry shout which was sure to call forth an equally merry answer from the people in the cars.

Often the friendly farmers would come to the doors to see them pass. Once they met a boy on the road and he asked for a ride to his home, half a mile away.

"Yes, jump in," said Mr. Bobbsey, and the boy got in and was taken to his house almost before he knew it.

"Much obliged," he said on leaving them. "I live in the country but this is the first sleigh ride

I've ever had. Thanks a lot," and he took off his hat at parting.

Before noon Dalton was reached and they drove up to the home of Mr. Ramdell, an old family friend. Immediately Bob Ramdell, a boy of sixteen, rushed eagerly out to greet Bert.

"I'm glad you've come," he cried. "I've been watching for you for an hour."

"We made pretty good time," answered Bert. "It isn't noon yet."

They went into the house while Sam drove the sleigh around to the barn. Bob Ramdell had a sister Susie, who was almost Nan's age, and a baby brother called Tootsie, although his real name was Alexander. Susie was glad to see Nan and Flossie, and soon all were playing with the baby, who was just old enough to be amusing.

"I've got something planned for us," whispered Bob to Bert, just before dinner was served. "I wonder if your father will let us carry it out."

"What is it?" questioned Bert.

"You won't be starting for home until late this afternoon. I wonder if your father will let you go down to Long Lake with me after dinner, to see the hockey match."

"Is it far from here?"

"About two miles. We can drive down in our car. Father will let me drive if I go slowly."

"I'll ask Dad," said Bert. "I'd like to see the hockey match very much."

As soon as he got the chance, Bert questioned his father about going with Bob.

"I don't know about this," said Mr. Bobbsey slowly. "Do you think you two boys can be trusted alone with Mr. Ramdell's car in the snow?"

"Oh, yes, Dad. Bob has driven it many times."

Bert promised they would be careful, and in the end Mr. Bobbsey gave him permission to go to the hockey match.

"But you must be back before five o'clock," warned Bert's father. "We are going to start for home at that time."

The dinner was a fine one and tasted especially good to the children after their long ride. But Bert and Bob were impatient to be off, and left the moment they had finished their pumpkin pie.

The distance to Long Lake was covered almost before Bert knew it. As the hockey game had not yet begun, they spent half an hour in driving over the road that led around the lake.

Quite a crowd had gathered, some in cars and some on foot, and the surface of the lake was covered with skaters. When the hockey game started the crowd watched every move with interest.

It was a "hot" game, according to Bert, and

when a clever play was made he yelled and cheered as loudly as the rest. However, there were many delays in the game. It almost seemed as though there were more arguments between the teams than there were plays. Several times Bert had to ask the man standing next to him what time it was. He told the man they had to go home at four-thirty.

"We must get back on time," he said to Bob. "I promised to be back at your house at five."

"Oh, we'll get there in no time," said Bob.

At the most exciting moment of the game, just when one of the players had been struck on the forehead with a hockey stick, Bert's neighbor told him it was time to leave.

Reluctantly the boys started for the car, turning to watch the game as long as possible. They were about halfway home and making good time when an ominous whistling came from the right rear wheel.

"Oh—oh," said Bob. "There goes one of our tires."

He brought the car to a stop at a level spot where a driveway joined the road.

"What'll we do?" asked Bert, thinking of his promise to be home by five o'clock.

"Don't you worry, Bert," said Bob, jumping out. "It won't take a minute to change that tire."

In no time at all he had the jack out of the rear compartment. While he was jacking up the axle, he showed Bert how to unfasten the bolts on the wheel.

A few minutes later the spare wheel was put on, the tools quickly replaced in the trunk, and they were on their way again.

Bert admired Bob's ability to change wheels so quickly. He was sure they would make the house by five o'clock after all, and they did!

CHAPTER XVII

BERT'S BLACK EYE

NOT long after Grace Lavine's party, Nan came down to breakfast looking very pale and worried.

"What is the trouble, Nan?" questioned Mrs. Bobbsey. "What has happened?"

"Oh, Mother, I can't tell you," answered Nan. "I'm afraid you'll laugh at me."

"I think you'd better tell me," said Mrs. Bobbsey. "I won't laugh."

"I saw the ghost last night—or rather, early this morning."

"What, the ghost that I saw?" shouted Bert.

"I think it must have been the same. Anyway, it was about that high"—Nan raised her hand to her shoulder—"and all pure white."

"Oh, Nan!" shivered Freddie. "Don't want any ghostses!"

"I don't want to see it," put in Flossie, and edged closer to her mother as if fearful the ghost might walk into the dining room that very minute.

"This is certainly strange," exclaimed Mr. Bobbsey. "Tell us all about it, Nan!"

"Oh, Daddy, you won't laugh?" Nan's face grew very red. "I—I—didn't think of it then, but it must have been very funny," she continued.

"It's not very funny to think you see a ghost, Nan," said Mrs. Bobbsey.

"I didn't mean that—I mean that I did afterward. You see I was asleep and I woke up all of a sudden, for I thought somebody had passed a hand over my face." She shivered a little. "All of a sudden I saw the ghost—it was standing right in front of the bureau," continued Nan. "I could see into the glass and for a moment I thought there were two ghosts."

"Oh!" came from Flossie. "Two! Wasn't that simply dreadful!" And she crouched closer than ever to her mother.

"As I was looking, the ghost moved away toward the window and then I saw there was only one. I was so scared I couldn't call anybody."

"I believe you," said Bert. "It's awful, isn't it?"

"This is certainly strange," said Mr. Bobbsey, with a grave look on his face. "What did you do next, Nan?"

"You—you won't laugh, Daddy?"

"No."

"I thought of my ski poles. They were resting against the wall, close to the bed. I turned over and reached for one, but it slipped down and made a terrible noise as it struck the floor. Then I flung the covers over my head."

"What did you want the ski pole for?" questioned Freddie, in great wonder. "You weren't going skiing."

"I thought I could—could stick the ghost with it," faltered Nan.

At this Bert could contain himself no longer, and he set up a shout of laughter, which was instantly repressed by Mr. Bobbsey.

"Oh, Nan, I'm sorry I laughed," said her twin brother, when he could speak. "But the idea of your poking at a ghost with a ski pole!"

"It was more than you tried to do," said Mr. Bobbsey dryly.

"That is true." Bert grew red in the face. "Did you see the ghost after that?" he asked, to hide his confusion.

"No."

"Not at all?" asked Mrs. Bobbsey.

"No, Mother. I stayed under the covers for about a minute—just like Bert did—and when I looked, the ghost was gone."

"I will have to investigate this," said Mr. Bobbsey seriously. "It is queer that neither your mother nor I has seen the ghost."

"I haven't seen it," said Flossie.

"Don't want to see it," piped up Freddie.

Dinah, in the kitchen, had heard Nan's story and she was scared almost to death.

"That is the strangest thing," she said to Sam, when he came for his breakfast. "What do you make of it?"

"Dunno," said Sam. "Maybe it means trouble."

The matter was talked over by the Bobbsey family several times that day.

"I'll sit up tonight and watch for that ghost," said Mr. Bobbsey. "If he shows up—well, he'll wish he hadn't, that's all."

"Oh, aren't you afraid?" asked Nan.

"Not a bit of it—nothing to be afraid of," answered her father.

True to his word, Mr. Bobbsey sat up all night waiting for the ghost. He had Bert's baseball bat by his side. But he did not have a chance to use it, for the ghost did not appear.

"I think the children must have been dreaming about that ghost," he said at breakfast.

"I will watch tonight," said Mrs. Bobbsey.

"Oh, Mother, be careful!" cried Nan with a shiver.

"I am not afraid," declared her mother.

Mrs. Bobbsey sat up all night, reading and listening, and did not fall asleep until the sun was coming up.

"I saw no ghost—nor did I hear one," she declared.

"Maybe the ghost saw you first and hid away," suggested Bert.

At this Mrs. Bobbsey laughed.

"Sam can try it tonight," she said. "Maybe he'll have better luck than Daddy or I."

When Dinah heard that her husband was going to sit up and watch for the ghost, she was very fearful and rolled her eyes in alarm.

"You be careful, Sam," she said. "Don't you let no ghost spirit you away!"

"Ain't no ghost goin' to touch me!" declared Sam. "That is, not if I see him first!"

"Would you kill him?" asked Freddie.

"I sure would. Ghosts better not prowl 'round this fella. I'll take Bert's bat and knock that ghost's head for a home run!"

"But you can't kill a ghost," insisted Nan. "Why, the fairy stories say you can see right through them!"

"That's the reason they are called fairy stories," declared her father. "Because they are not true. There is no such thing as a ghost. It's only some thing make-believe."

All night long Sam sat in the upper hall in a rocking chair. Several times he dozed off, but he declared that he heard everything, nevertheless.

"An' there wasn't no ghost—not one speck of one," declared Sam.

At this Mr. and Mrs. Bobbsey shook their heads in perplexity and both looked at their older daughter.

"Perhaps you were dreaming, Nan," said Mrs. Bobbsey.

"No, I wasn't dreaming, Mother, and Bert says he wasn't dreaming, either."

"It is strange. I cannot understand it at all."

"Do you believe in ghosts, Mother?"

"No, my dear."

"But I saw something."

"Perhaps it was only a reflection. Sometimes the street lights throw strange shadows on the walls through the windows."

"It wasn't a shadow," said Nan. And there the talk ended, for Mrs. Bobbsey did not know what to say to comfort her daughter.

In some way the news that a ghost had been seen in the Bobbsey house spread throughout the neighborhood, and many came to ask about it. The boys and girls talked about it and asked Nan and Bert all manner of questions, most of which the twins could not answer.

The "ghost talk," as it was called, gave Danny Rugg a good chance to annoy both Nan and Bert.

"Afraid of a ghost! Afraid of a ghost!" he would cry, whenever he saw them. "Oh my, Bert and Nan are afraid of a ghost!"

"I think it is perfectly dreadful," said Nan one day, on returning from school. Her eyes were red, showing that she had been crying.

"I'll 'ghost' him, if he yells at us again," said Bert. "I'm not going to stand it, so there!"

"But what will you do, Bert?"

"I'll fight him, that's what I'll do."

"Oh, Bert, you mustn't fight."

"Then he has got to leave you alone—and leave me alone, too."

"If you fight at school, you'll be expelled."

"I don't care, I'm going to make him mind his own business," said Bert recklessly.

Danny Rugg was particularly jealous because he had not been invited to Grace Lavine's party. Of all the boys in that neighborhood he was the only one left out, and he fancied it was Nan's and Bert's fault.

"They don't like me and they are setting everybody against me," he thought. "I won't stand for it, not me!"

Two days later he followed Bert into the schoolyard, in which a large number of boys were playing.

"Hi! How's your ghost?" he cried. "Is it still living at your house?"

"You forget about that ghost, Danny Rugg!" cried Bert, his eyes flashing.

"Oh, but wouldn't I like to have a house with a ghost," went on Danny tantalizingly. "And a sister who was afraid of it!"

"Will you stop it, or not?"

"Why should I stop? You've got the ghost, haven't you? And Nan is scared to death of it, isn't she?"

"No, she isn't."

"Yes she is, and so are you and all the rest of the family." And then Danny set up his old shout: "Afraid of a ghost! Afraid of a ghost!"

Some of the other boys followed suit and soon a dozen or more were crying, "Afraid of a ghost!" as loudly as they could.

Bert grew very pale and his breath came thickly. He watched Danny and when he came closer, caught him by the arm.

"Let go!" cried the big boy roughly.

"I want you to cut it out."

"I won't."

"Oh, yes, you will!"

Bert had hardly spoken when Danny struck at him and hit him on the arm. Then Bert struck back and hit Danny on the chin. A dozen or more blows followed in quick succession. One struck Bert in the eye and blackened it, and another reached Danny's nose and made it bleed. Then the two boys clinched and rolled over on the schoolyard pavement.

"A fight! A fight!" shouted the others. In a minute a crowd had gathered to see what was going on.

The school principal, Mr. Tetlow, was just entering the school at the front. Hearing the cry, he ran around into the yard.

"Boys! Boys! Stop at once!" he demanded, and forced his way through the crowd to where Bert and Danny lay, still pommeling each other. "Stand up and behave yourselves," he ordered sternly. Reaching down, he caught each boy by the collar and dragged him to his feet.

CHAPTER XVIII

NAN'S PLEA

BERT'S heart sank when he saw that it was the school principal who held him by the collar. He remembered what Nan had said about fighting and being expelled.

"It was Bert Bobbsey's fault," blustered Danny, wiping his bleeding nose on his sleeve.

"No, it wasn't," answered Bert quickly. "It was Danny's fault."

"I say it was your fault!" shouted Danny. "He started the fight, Mr. Tetlow."

"He hit me first," went on Bert, undaunted.

"He caught me by the arm and wouldn't let me go," came from Danny.

"I told him to keep still," explained Bert. "He was calling, 'Afraid of a ghost!' at me and I don't like it. And he said my sister Nan was afraid of it, too."

"Both of you march up to my office," said

Mr. Tetlow sternly. "And remain there until I come."

"My nose is bleeding," whined Danny.

"You may go and wash the blood away first," said the principal.

With a heart that was exceedingly heavy, Bert entered the school and made his way to the principal's office. No one was there, and he sank into a chair in a corner. He heard the bells ring and heard the pupils enter the school and go to their various classrooms.

"If I am sent home, what will Mother and Daddy say?" he thought dismally. He had never yet been sent home for misconduct, and the very idea filled him with nameless dread.

His blackened eye began to throb a bit, too, but this did not bother him nearly as much as the thought of what Mr. Tetlow would have to say when he came in.

Presently the door opened and Danny shuffled in, a wet and bloody handkerchief held to his nose. He sat down on the opposite side of the office, and for several minutes nothing was said by either of the boys.

"I suppose you are going to try to get me into trouble," said Danny at length.

"You're trying to get me into trouble," re,

turned Bert. "I didn't start the quarrel, and you know it."

"I don't know anything of the kind, Bert Bobbsey! If you say I started the fight—I'll—I'll—tell something more about you."

"Really?"

"Yes, really."

"What can you tell?"

"You know well enough. Mr. Ringley hasn't forgotten about his broken window."

"Well, you broke that. I didn't."

"Huh! If I say *you* broke it, how can you prove you didn't?"

"Danny Rugg, what do you mean?" exclaimed Bert. "You know I had nothing to do with that broken window."

The big boy was about to say something more in reply when Mr. Tetlow entered the office.

"Boys," he said abruptly, "this is a disgraceful affair. I thought both of you knew better than to fight. It is setting a very bad example to the rest of the students. I shall have to punish you both severely."

Mr. Tetlow paused and Bert's heart leaped into his throat. What if he should be expelled? The very thought of it made him shiver.

"I have made a number of inquiries of the

other pupils, and I find that you, Danny, started the quarrel. You raised the cry of 'Afraid of a ghost!' when you had no right to do so, and when Bert caught you by the arm and told you to stop you struck him. Is this true?"

"I—I—he hit me in the chin. I told him to let me go."

"He struck me first, Mr. Tetlow," put in Bert. "I am sure all the boys will say the same."

"Hem! Bert, you can go to your classroom. I will talk to you after school this afternoon."

Somewhat relieved, Bert left the office and walked to the classroom, where the other pupils eyed him curiously, especially his swollen eye which had now taken on a purple hue. It was hard work to put his mind on his lessons, but he did his best, for he did not wish to miss in any of them and thus make matters worse.

"What did the principal do?" whispered the boy who sat next to him.

"Hasn't done anything yet," whispered Bert.

"It was Danny's fault," went on the boy. "We'll stick by you."

At noontime Bert walked home with Nan, feeling very much downcast.

"Oh, Bert, I begged you not to fight," said his twin sister.

"I couldn't help it, Nan. He told everybody that you were afraid of the ghost."

"And what is Mr. Tetlow going to do?"

"I don't know. He told me to stay in after school this afternoon, as he wanted to talk with me."

"If he expels you, Mother will never get over it."

"I know that, Nan. But—but—I couldn't stand it to have him yelling out, 'Afraid of a ghost!'"

After that Nan said little. But her thoughts were busy, and by the time they were returning to the school, her mind was fully made up.

To all of the school children the principal's office was a place that usually filled them with awe. Rarely did anybody go there, except when sent by a teacher on an errand, or because of some infringements of the rules.

Nan went to school early that afternoon, and as soon as she had left Bert and the two younger twins, she marched bravely to Mr. Tetlow's office and knocked on the door.

"Come in," said the principal, who was at his desk looking over some school reports.

"If you please, Mr. Tetlow, I came to see you about my brother, Bert Bobbsey," began Nan.

Mr. Tetlow looked at her kindly, for he half expected what was coming.

"What is it, Nan?" he asked.

"I—I—oh, Mr. Tetlow, won't you please let Bert off this time? He only did it because Danny said such things about me; said I was afraid of the ghost, and made all the boys call out that we had ghosts at our house. I—I—think, somehow, that I ought to be punished if he is."

There, it was out, and Nan felt better for it. Her deep brown eyes looked squarely into the eyes of the principal.

In spite of himself Mr. Tetlow was compelled to smile. He knew something of how devoted the Bobbsey twins were to each other.

"So you think you ought to be punished," he said slowly.

"Yes, if Bert is, for you see, he did it mostly for me."

"You are a brave sister to come in his behalf, Nan. I shall not punish him very severely."

"Oh, thank you for saying that, Mr. Tetlow."

"It was very wrong for him to fight—"

"Yes, I told him that."

"But Danny Rugg did wrong to provoke him. I sincerely trust that both boys forgive each other for what was done. Now you may go."

With a lighter heart Nan left the office. She felt that Bert would not be expelled. And he was not. Instead, Mr. Tetlow made him stay in an hour after school each day that week and write on the blackboard the sentence, "Fighting is wrong," a hundred times.

Danny also was kept in and was made to write the sentence just twice as many times. Then Mr. Tetlow made the two boys shake hands and promise to behave better in the future.

The punishment was nothing to what Bert had expected, and he stayed in after school willingly. But Danny was very sulky and plotted all manner of evil things against the Bobbseys.

"He is a very bad boy," said Nan. "If I were you, Bert, I'd have nothing more to do with him."

"I don't intend to have anything to do with him," answered her twin brother. "But, Nan, what do you think he meant when he said he'd make trouble about Mr. Ringley's broken window? Do you imagine he'll tell Mr. Ringley I broke it?"

"How would he dare, when he broke it himself?" burst out Nan.

"I'm sure I don't know. But if he did, what do you suppose Mr. Ringley would do?"

"I don't know," Nan said helplessly. "You

can't prove that Danny really did it, can you?"

"No."

"It's too bad. I wish the window hadn't been broken."

"So do I," said Bert. And there the talk came to an end, for there seemed nothing more to say.

CHAPTER XIX

ST. VALENTINE'S DAY

ST. VALENTINE'S DAY was now close at hand, and all the children of the neighborhood were saving their money to buy valentines.

"I know just the ones I am going to get," said Nan.

"I want some big red hearts," cried Freddie. "Just love hearts, I do!"

"I want the kind you can look into," said Flossie. "You know, the kind that fold up."

Two days before St. Valentine's Day the children gathered around the dining-room table and began to make valentines. They had paper of various colors and pictures cut from old magazines. They worked very hard, and some of the valentines were as attractive as any sold in the stores.

"Oh, I saw just the valentine for Freddie," whispered Nan to Bert. "It had a picture of a fireman running to a fire on it."

There were a great many mysterious sealed envelopes to be posted in the Bobbsey house on the afternoon before St. Valentine's Day, and Mr. Bobbsey had to supply quite a few postage stamps.

"My, my, but the postman will have a lot to do tomorrow," said Mr. Bobbsey. "If this keeps on, I'm afraid he'll want his salary raised."

The fun began early in the morning. On coming down to breakfast each of the children found a valentine under his or her plate. They were all very pretty.

"Where in the world did they come from?" cried Nan. "Oh, Mother, did you put them there?"

"No, Nan," said Mrs. Bobbsey.

"Then it must have been Dinah!" said Nan, and rushed into the kitchen. "Oh, Dinah, how good of you!"

"I expect they're from St. Valentine," said the cook, smiling broadly.

"Oh, I know you!" said Nan.

"Look at mine!" cried Freddie. "Mine's a girl and her eyes roll 'round and 'round."

The postman came just before it was time to start for school. He brought six valentines, three for Flossie, two for Freddie and one for Bert.

"Oh, Nan, where is yours?" asked Bert.

"I—I guess he forgot me," said Nan quietly.

"He must have made a mistake," said Bert, and ran after the postman. But it was no use—all the mail for the Bobbseys had been delivered.

"Never mind, he'll come again this afternoon," said Mrs. Bobbsey, who saw how disappointed Nan was.

On her desk in school Nan found several valentines from her schoolmates. They were all very pretty except one, which was homemade. It was a drawing of a girl running away from a white figure labeled GHOST. Nan put this out of sight as soon as she saw it.

All that day valentines were being delivered in various ways. Freddie found one in his cap, and there was one for Bert between the leaves of his geography book. Flossie found a valentine pinned to her coat, and Nan received one in a cardboard box labeled Breakfast Food. It was made of paper roses and was very pretty.

The postman came that afternoon just as they arrived home from school. This time he had three valentines for Nan and several for the others. Most of them were comical, but some were very beautiful and contained very affectionate verses. There was much guessing as to who had sent them.

"I have received just as many as I sent out," said Nan, counting them over.

"I sent out two more than I received," said Bert.

"Never mind, Bert: boys don't expect so many as girls," answered Nan.

"I'd like to know who sent that mean one that was marked GHOST," said her twin brother with a scowl.

"It must have come from Danny Rugg," answered Nan. She was right. It had come from Danny, but Nan never let him know that she had received it, so his hoped-for fun over it was spoiled.

In the evening there was more fun than ever. All of the children went out and dropped valentines on the front porches of their friends' houses. As soon as a valentine was dropped, the doorbell would be given a sharp ring, and then everybody would run and hide and watch to see who came to the door.

When the Bobbsey children went home, they saw somebody on their own front porch. It was a boy and he was on his knees, placing something under the door mat.

"I believe it is Danny Rugg!" cried Nan.

"Wait, I'll go and catch him," said Bert, and started forward.

But Danny saw him coming, and leaping over the side rail of the porch, he ran to the back garden.

"Stop," ordered Bert. "I know you, Danny Rugg!"

"I'm not Danny Rugg!" shouted Danny in a rough voice. "I'm somebody else."

He continued to run and Bert took after him. At last Danny reached the back fence. There was a gate there, but this was kept locked by Sam, so that peddlers could not get in.

For the moment Danny did not know what to do. Then he caught hold of the top of the fence and tried to scramble over. But there was a sharp nail there and on this his jacket caught.

"I've got you now!" exclaimed Bert, and made a grab for him. There followed the sound of ripping cloth and Danny disappeared into the darkness, wearing a jacket that had a big hole in it.

"Was it really Danny?" asked Nan, when Bert came back to the front porch.

"Yes, and he tore his coat—I heard it rip."

"Bert, look! What do you think of that?"

Nan pointed to an object on the porch half under the door mat. There lay a dead rat, and around its neck was a string to which was attached a card reading, "Nan and Bert Bobbsey's Ghost."

"That's Danny Rugg for you."

"This is certainly awful," said Bert. "He's the meanest boy in the whole class."

The noise on the porch had brought Mrs. Bobbsey to the door. At the sight of the dead rat, which Freddie had calmly picked up by the tail, she gave a slight scream.

"Oh, Freddie, put it down!" she cried.

"It won't hurt you, Mommy," said the little boy. "The real is gone out of it."

"But—but—how did it get here?"

"Danny Rugg brought it," said Bert. "Look at the tag."

He cut the tag off with his pocketknife and flung the rat into the garbage can. Then they went into the house and Mrs. Bobbsey and her husband both read what Danny Rugg had written on the card.

"This is going too far," said Mr. Bobbsey. "I must speak to Mr. Rugg about this."

Mr. Bobbsey telephoned to Mr. Rugg the next day and told him about the rat. As a result, and because of the jacket, Danny received the hardest thrashing he had got in a year.

This made him more angry than ever at Bert,

and also angry with the whole Bobbsey family. But he did not dare do anything to hurt them right away, for fear of getting caught.

Winter was now going fast, and before long the signs of spring began to show. Buds appeared on the trees, and the grass started to turn green.

Spring made Freddie think of a big kite that he had stored away in the garret, and one Saturday he and Bert got the kite out and fixed the string and the tail.

"There is a good breeze blowing," said Bert. "Let's go and fly it on Roscoe's field."

"I want to see you fly the kite," said Flossie. "May I go along?"

"Sure, come on," said Bert.

Flossie had been playing with the kitten and hated to leave it. So she went down to the field with Snoop in her arms.

"Don't let Snoop run away from you," said Bert. "He might not find his way back home."

The field was a large one with an old barn at one end. Freddie and Bert took the kite to one end. Freddie held it up while Bert prepared to let out the string and "run it up," as he called it.

Now, as it happened, the eyes of Snoop were fixed on the long tail of the kite, and when it went trailing over the ground, Snoop leaped from Flossie's arms and made a dash for it. The kitten's claws caught fast in the tail, and in a moment more the kite went up into the air and Snoop with it!

"Oh, my kitten!" screamed Freddie. "Snoop has gone up with the kite!"

CHAPTER XX

SNOOP IS RESCUED

BERT kept on running across the field, not re-
alizing that poor Snoop was dangling on the end
of the kite's tail. Both Flossie and Freddie set
up a loud cry of fear.

"Snoop will be killed!" exclaimed the little
girl. "Oh, poor, dear Snoop!" And she wrung
her hands in despair.

"Bert, stop!" shouted Freddie. "Snoop's up in
the sky!"

But Bert did not hear them and kept running
toward the barn. A strong gust of wind caught
the kite. It rocked from side to side with poor
Snoop still caught on the tail. The kitten wailed
with fright.

"Get him down!" shrieked Freddie. "Oh,
Bert, please get my kitten down, won't you?"

Bert at last heard Freddie and turned around.

"Hey, what's on the tail?" he yelled. "Is that
—Snoop?"

"Oh, Bert," called Freddie, who was rushing up to his big brother. "Do let him down. If he falls, he'll be killed!"

"Don't worry, Freddie," Bert answered. "I'll get Snoop down." He started to pull in on the string.

The kite gradually began to settle close to the top of the old barn. Poor Snoop was swinging violently at the end of the ragged tail. The swinging brought the frightened creature closer still to the barn. All of a sudden Snoop let go the tail of the kite and landed on the roof.

"Snoop is on top of the barn!" cried Bert, as the kite settled on the grass a few yards away.

"Oh, Snoop! Snoop! Are you hurt?" cried Freddie, running back a distance, so that he might get a view of the barn roof.

Evidently Snoop was not hurt. But he was still scared, for he stood on the edge of the roof, with his tail standing straight up.

"Meow, meow, meow!" he said plaintively.

"He is asking for somebody to take him down," said Freddie. "Aren't you, Snoop?"

"Meow!" answered the black kitten.

"Oh, dear me, what will you do now?" cried Flossie, as she came rushing up.

"Perhaps I can get to the roof from the inside," said Bert, darting quickly into the barn.

There was a rickety pair of stairs leading to the barn loft, which he mounted. In the loft all was dark and full of cobwebs. Here and there were small holes in the roof, through which the water came every time it rained.

"Snoop! Snoop!" he called, putting his mouth close to one of the holes.

The kitten turned around in surprise. He hardly knew from where the voice came, but he evidently knew Bert was calling, for he soon came in that direction.

As the barn was an old one and had not been used in years, Bert felt it would do no harm to knock a shingle or two from the roof. Looking around, he spied an old broom handle lying on the floor and with this he began an attack on the shingles and soon had two of them broken away.

"Come, Snoop!" he called, looking out the hole. "Come here!"

But the sound of the blows had frightened the kitten, and Snoop had fled to the slope of the roof on the opposite side of the barn.

"Where is he?" called the boy to the twins below.

"Gone to the other side," said Freddie. "Doesn't like the noise, I guess."

"Chase him over here," returned Bert.

Both Freddie and Flossie tried to do so. But

Snoop would not budge. He just stood on the very edge of the roof, as if meditating a spring to the ground.

"Don't jump, please don't jump, Snoop!" pleaded Flossie. "If you jump, you'll surely break a leg, or maybe your back!"

Whether Snoop understood this or not, it would be hard to say. But he did not jump. He just stayed where he was and meowed louder than ever.

"Can't you drive him over?" asked Bert, after a long wait.

"Won't come," said Freddie. "Wants to jump down, I guess."

Hearing this, Bert ran down to the lower floor and outside.

"Can't you get a ladder?" asked Flossie. "Perhaps Mr. Roscoe will lend you one."

Mr. Roscoe's house was at the other end of the field. He was a very old and very quiet man, and most of the girls and boys in Lakeport were afraid of him. He lived all alone and was thought to be queer.

"I—I can find out," said Bert hesitatingly.

He ran across the field to Mr. Roscoe's house and rapped on the door. Nobody came, so he rapped again, and then a third time.

"Who's there?" asked a voice from within.

"Please, Mr. Roscoe, is that you?" asked Bert.
"Yes."

"Well, our kitten is on the top of your old barn and can't get down. Can you lend me a ladder to get him down with?"

"Kitten on my barn? How did he get there?" The old man opened the door slowly and cautiously. He had white hair and was bent with age.

"He went up with a kite," said Bert, and told the whole story, to which the old man listened with interest.

"Well! well! well!" exclaimed Mr. Roscoe, in a high, piping voice. "Going to take a sail through the air, was he? You'll have to build him a helicopter, eh?"

"I think he had better stay on the ground after this."

"He must be a high-flyer of a cat." And the old man chuckled over his joke.

"Will you lend me a ladder?" went on Bert.

"Certainly, my lad. The ladder is in the tool shed yonder. But you'll have to raise it yourself, or get somebody to raise it for you. My back is too old and stiff for such work."

"I'll try it alone first," answered the boy. "Thank you, sir."

He soon had the long ladder out and was dragging it across the field. It was very heavy and he wondered whom he could get to help him raise it. Just then Danny Rugg came along.

"What are you doing with old Roscoe's ladder?" he asked.

Bert was on the point of telling Danny it was none of his business, but he paused and reflected. He wanted no more quarrels with the big boy.

"I am going to get our cat down from the barn roof," he answered.

"Humph!"

"Help me raise the ladder, will you, Danny?"

"Me? Not much! You can raise your own ladder."

"All right, I will, if you don't want to help me," said Bert, the blood rushing to his face.

"So that's your cat, is it?" cried Danny, looking toward the barn. "I wouldn't have that black thing! We've got a real Maltese at our house."

"We like Snoop!" answered Bert, and went on with his ladder.

Danny hunted for a stone, and watching his chance, threw it at Snoop. It landed close to the kitten, and made poor Snoop run to the other side of the barn roof.

"Stop that, Danny Rugg!" cried a voice from the other end of the field, and Nan appeared.

She had just heard about what had happened

to Snoop and was hurrying to the spot to see if she could help Bert.

"Oh, go on with your old cat!" sneered Danny, and he shuffled off past Mr. Roscoe's house.

The old man had come out to see how Bert was getting along with the ladder, and now he came face to face with Danny Rugg.

"Well, is it possible!" murmured the old man to himself. "That boy must belong around here after all!"

When Bert reached the barn, he found a dozen boys collected, and several volunteered to assist him in raising the long ladder. It was hard work, and once the ladder slipped, but in the end it rested against the barn roof and then Bert went up in a hurry.

"Come, Snoop!" he called, and the kitten came running across the shingles and perched himself on Bert's shoulder.

When Bert came down the ladder, those standing around set up a cheer, and Freddie and Flossie clapped their hands in delight.

"Oh, I'm so glad you got him back!" said Freddie and hugged the kitten almost to death.

"What boy was that who threw the stone?" asked Mr. Roscoe of Nan, while Bert was returning the ladder to the tool shed.

"That was Danny Rugg," answered Nan. "He is a bad boy."

"I know he is a bad boy," said Mr. Roscoe. "A very bad boy indeed." And then the old man hurried off without another word. What he said meant a good deal, as we shall soon see.

CHAPTER XXI

A MYSTERY SOLVED

THE rescue of the kitten was the main subject of conversation that evening in the Bobbsey household.

"I never dreamed he would go up with the kite," said Flossie. "After this, we'll have to keep him in the house when Bert and Freddie do their kite flying."

Bert had seen Danny Rugg throw the stone at the kitten and was very angry. He had also seen Danny talk to Nan.

"I think he's an awful boy," declared Nan. "And Mr. Roscoe thinks he is bad, too."

"He had better stop throwing things or he'll get himself into trouble before long," said Bert.

"It's queer Mr. Ringley never heard who broke the window," whispered his twin sister.

"So it is. But it may come out yet," replied her brother.

In early June the Bobbseys had their first

strawberry shortcake of the season. It was a beautiful cake—one of Dinah's best—and the strawberries were large and luscious.

"Want another piece," said Freddie, smacking his lips. "It's so good, Mommy!"

"Freddie, I think you have had enough," said Mrs. Bobbsey.

"Oh, Mommy, just a little piece more!" pleaded Freddie, and received the piece, much to his satisfaction.

"Strawberries are beautiful," he declared. "I'm going to raise a whole lot on the farm this summer."

"Oh, Mother, are we going to Uncle Dan's farm this summer?" cried Nan eagerly.

"Perhaps, Nan," replied Mrs. Bobbsey. "I expect a letter very shortly."

"Meadow Brook is a dandy place," said Bert. "Such a fine swimming hole in the brook!"

"Oh, I love the flowers, and the chickens and cows!" said Flossie.

"I like the rides on the loads of hay," said Nan.

The children talked about the farm until it was time to go to bed. Their Uncle Dan and Aunt Sarah lived at Meadow Brook, and so did their cousin Harry, a boy a little older than Bert, and one who was full of fun and very good-natured in the bargain.

Bert went to bed with his head full of plans for the summer. What glorious times they could have after school closed, if they went to their uncle's farm!

It was a full hour before Bert got to sleep. The room was quite bright, for the moon was shining in the corner window. The moon made him think of the ghost he had once seen and he gave a little shudder. He never wanted to see that ghost again.

Bert had been asleep less than an hour when he awoke with a start. He felt sure somebody had touched him on the foot. He opened his eyes at once and looked toward the end of his bed.

The ghost was standing there!

At first Bert could scarcely believe what he saw. But it was true, and he promptly dived under the covers.

Then he thought of Danny Rugg's cry, "Afraid of a ghost!" and he felt that he ought to have more courage.

"I'm going to see what that is," he said to himself, and shoved back the covers once more.

The figure in white had moved toward the corner of the room. It made no noise and Bert wondered which way it would turn next.

"Wonder what will happen if I grab it, or yell?" he asked himself.

With equal silence Bert crawled out of bed. Close at hand stood his baseball bat. It made a formidable club, and he took hold of it with a good deal of satisfaction.

"Want another piece of strawberry shortcake," came to his ears. "Please give me another piece of strawberry shortcake."

Bert could hardly believe his ears. It was the ghost that was speaking! It wanted strawberry shortcake!

"Freddie!" he whispered. "Freddie, is it you?"

The ghost did not answer, but turned toward the door leading into the hallway. Bert ran after the figure in white and caught up with it.

The ghost was really Freddie, and he was walking in his sleep, with his eyes tightly closed.

"Well, what do you know!" murmured Bert. "Why didn't we think of this before?"

"Please let me have another piece of strawberry shortcake, Mommy," pleaded the sleepwalker. "Just a tiny little piece."

Bert had heard that it was a bad thing to awaken a sleepwalker too suddenly, so he took Freddie's arm very gently and walked the little fellow back to his bedroom and helped him into bed. Then he shook him very gently.

"Oh!" cried Freddie. "Oh! Wha—what do

you want? Let me sleep! It isn't time to get up yet."

"Freddie, I want you to wake up," said Bert.

"Who is talking?" came from across the hall-way, in Mr. Bobbsey's voice.

"I am, Dad," answered Bert. He ran to the doorway of his father's bedroom. "I've just found out who the ghost is," he continued.

"The ghost?" Mr. Bobbsey leaped up. "Where is it?"

"In bed now. It was Freddie, walking in his sleep. He was asking for another piece of straw-berry shortcake."

By this time the whole household was wide awake.

"Oh, Freddie, was it really you?" cried Nan, going to the little fellow.

"Wasn't walking in my sleep," said Freddie. "Was dreaming 'bout shortcake, that's all. Want to go to sleep again," and he turned over on his pillow.

"Let him sleep," said Mrs. Bobbsey. "We'll have to consult the doctor about this. Freddie probably has nothing seriously wrong. He must eat less before going to bed."

The next day the doctor was called in, and he gave Freddie some medicine which ended the little boy's sleepwalking to a very large extent.

"I am glad you caught Freddie," said Nan to her twin brother. "If you hadn't, I should always have believed that we had seen a ghost."

"Glad I don't walk in my sleep," said Flossie. "I might tumble downstairs and break my nose."

"I shall watch Freddie in the future," said Mrs. Bobbsey, and she did.

When Bert went to school the next day he met Danny Rugg and the tall boy glared at him very angrily.

"Think you are smart, don't you?" said Danny. "I'm not going to stand for it, Bert Bobbsey."

"Oh, Bert, come along and don't speak to him," whispered Nan, who was with her twin brother.

"Went and saw Ringley, didn't you?" went on Danny, edging closer.

"Keep away, Danny Rugg," answered Bert. "I want nothing to do with you, and I haven't been to see Mr. Ringley."

"Yes, you did go and see him," insisted Danny. "Wasn't he in to see my father last night?"

"Did Mr. Ringley come to see your father?" asked Bert curiously.

"Yes, he did. And my father—but never mind that now," broke off the tall boy. He had been on the point of saying that his father had given him a severe thrashing. "I'm going to fix you, Bert Bobbsey."

"Don't you dare strike my brother, Danny Rugg!" warned Nan, stepping in between them.

How much further the quarrel might have gone, it is impossible to say, for just then Mr. Tetlow put in an appearance, and Danny sneaked off in great haste.

Later, when the children came home from school, they learned that Mrs. Bobbsey had been downtown, buying some shoes for herself.

"Mr. Ringley was telling me about his broken window," she said to her husband that evening. "He found out that Danny Rugg broke it. Old Mr. Roscoe saw Danny do it. He didn't know Danny at the time, but he has found out since who Danny was."

"That Rugg boy is a bad one," answered Mr. Bobbsey. "I suppose Mr. Ringley made the Ruggs pay for the window."

"Oh, yes, and Mr. Rugg said he was going to punish Danny, too."

The children heard this talk, but said nothing at the time. Later Nan called Bert out into the garden.

"I see it all," she whispered to her twin

brother. "That's why Mr. Roscoe asked me who Danny was, and that's why he said Danny was such a bad boy."

"I'm glad in one way that Danny has been found out," answered Bert, "for that clears me." And he was right, for he never heard about the broken window again.

The children were still waiting anxiously for a letter from their Uncle Dan or their Aunt Sarah.

"What will we do if it doesn't come, Mother?" asked Nan.

"Then we'll go to some other farm," her mother replied.

"Oh, what do you think?" cried Nan, dancing up to Bert. "We are to go to the country as soon as vacation begins!"

"Good!" shouted Bert, throwing his cap into the air. "Won't we have the best times ever!"

And they certainly did. What happened to the Bobbsey twins during vacation will be told in "The Bobbsey Twins in the Country."

The country is a lovely place, especially in the summertime, and all children love to play in the fields and brooks and barns, just as the Bobbsey twins were going to do.

That evening, to celebrate the good news, the

twins gave a little party to half a dozen of their most intimate friends. They had music and singing, and all sorts of games, and a sleight-of-hand exhibit by one of the boys. All enjoyed it greatly and voted the little party a great success.

"Good night! Good night!" said the children to each other, when the party broke up. And here let us say good night, too, for this little story has reached its end.

Don't miss the next story—

THE BOBBSEY TWINS
IN THE COUNTRY